Steel City 4

Liberty Bridge Is Falling Down

A Sam Budda and Nick Savarese Novel

William Lafferty

New Image Press, Pittsburgh PA

BOOKS BY
WILLIAM LAFFERTY

• • •

The Claysville Escapade

The Warehouse on 49th Street

The Well-Heeled Rapist

Liberty Bridge Is Falling Down

Roxellana

After the Dogfights

They Came for Our Guns, They Came for Our Freedom

Death by Popular Vote: Betrayal From Within

• • •

See the website at
www.williamlafferty.com

New Image Press
4433 Howley Street
Pittsburgh, PA 15224

FIRST EDITION 2010
ISBN 978-0-9842963-3-0

• • • •

This book is dedicated to greed. It soils whatever it touches.

• • • •

Liberty Bridge Is Falling Down

CHAPTER ONE

It was 3:00 a.m. in early May. The temperature was in the forties. The sky was overcast and heavy. A drizzle came down. A white Cadillac STS approached the Liberty Bridge in downtown Pittsburgh. The car pulled to a stop at a traffic light on the ramp leading to the bridge. The driver, Tim Brannigan, lit a cigar as he waited for the light to turn. The windshield wipers cycled at four second intervals. A mist settled on the windshield in between cycles. The cigar caught and Tim replaced the cigarette lighter, puffing smoke and watching the light. To his right, the city glowed through a fog. "I don't know what I'm doing," he thought to himself, slumping in the seat in exhaustion.

Tim had been going since seven in the morning the day before. He'd been up for twenty hours. At five o'clock, ten hours ago, he had called his wife Janice to tell her he would be late. An emergency meeting at the accounting firm where he worked. One of his accounts was in trouble with the IRS.

IRS problems can go on for months, even years, but he couldn't use the same excuse forever. The truth was that for over a year Tim had been having an affair with Linda Girard, a cosmetics salesgirl he had met as he walked through a department store on his lunch break. He was smitten with her. He couldn't get enough of her. He'd lie forever if that's what it took to be with her.

Janice must know, he thought. Maybe she suspects. In some ways, as Tim absentmindedly stared at the mist surrounding the red light, Janice was just a distant memory, just someone he had to lie to. Just someone he had to avoid. Exhaustion was settling in. His mind was wandering. He couldn't keep doing this. He was going to be a zombie at work tomorrow. But he wasn't giving up Linda and nobody could afford a divorce. He'd take a nap tomorrow when he was working. He could sleep at the computer.

The light changed. The wipers cleared the windshield, giving him a fresh start, a new day. Everything was clean and clear. Tim was alone now on the long bridge, and the Cadillac began to roll. Its tires made a hissing noise on the wet pavement. Through the mist and the drizzle Tim saw the lights at the end of the bridge three hundred yards away, just in front of the tunnel. They were blinking yellow, so he wouldn't have to stop there. He could just drive right into the tunnel from the bridge.

But then the car jolted to the left. It almost seemed that it tilted. Tim was at first surprised and then alarmed. Had he hit something? A tire had blown on the left. No. Wait. Now the right side of the car was low. His side of the car seemed to be elevated. "I must have hit something, for Christ's sake," he cried to himself, irrationally. But there was nothing in the road.

As the car veered uncontrollably to the left and then to the right, he realized that streaks of light were moving across the horizon, high to low. The streaks started above the car and then disappeared below his line of sight. Then he realized what the streaks were. They were a hundred foot light poles falling off the edge of the bridge. Then other light poles fell on the bridge, crashing, sparking and exploding with a shattering display of glass and sparks.

The car was still veering wildly, unresponsive to the wheel and then there was a horrendous crack. It was as if lightning had struck right next to the car. And right after the crack, the car tilted menacingly to the left. The angle was so sharp that Tim thought he might spill out the door onto the pavement. But when he glanced out his side window, terror consumed him. There was no pavement. The road to his left was gone, and in its place was a jagged chasm and the black river rippling sixty feet below.

The bridge was split down the middle and the gap in the road was at least ten feet wide now. Tim glanced fearfully at the dark water gleaming, flowing with a quiet menace below. He slammed on the brakes, but the car continued to slide toward the chasm and the brakes seemed to have no effect at all.

Tim grabbed the wheel as if it were his salvation, the thing that would save him from death. But it was a false salvation. There was no hope. He was going to die. The noise became overwhelming as the bridge groaned, cracked and growled as it disintegrated. Steel bent, heated almost red hot, then snapped and concrete pillars exploded in clouds of cement dust. Rivets popped and then flew apart like bullets as the strain became more than they could hold. Tim's lane began to move upwards and then down to the left again. The car hung on the edge of the pavement, which now was tilting at an even more aggressive angle into the void. Tim looked out the side window and began to scream. In a desperate effort, he took his foot off the brake and floored the accelerator. The big V8 roared and hit redline as the wheels spun in mid-air.

The Cadillac hit the Monongahela River upside down with a terrific whop and with Tim, in shock, upside down suspended by his seat belt. The inverted car sat on the surface of the water momentarily, wheels in the air, its dark, oil-stained chassis facing the clouds. For a few seconds, the upside-down car bobbed on the surface, not moving and then slowly, gradually, it floated downstream, and as it floated, it sank, little by little, into the brown swirling water.

CHAPTER TWO

Janice Longstreet, later to be Tim's wife, was a girl without a purpose. She had gone to college to please her overbearing father and to get out from under the parental thumb, but college was just a waste of time for her. She had no interest in Western civilization, and she gradually drifted into the party girl syndrome that was favored by her sorority sisters. But even that was unsatisfying to her listless soul.

Then she met Tim Brannigan. Tim was her opposite. He was bright, enthusiastic, driven and cute. He was an accounting major and his ambition in life was to own his own accounting firm. He made her laugh and he helped her get through some of the more difficult classes she took just to be around him. Gradually, they began to spend all their time together and by their senior year, they were virtually living together, with Janice staying overnight at Tim's apartment most of the time. By the time of graduation, they decided to get married.

The wedding was a jumble of parents, Tim's friends, Janice's sorority sisters and somebody's kids carrying bouquets of flowers. The friends got up at the dinner and told sophomoric stories about the bride and groom, and the mothers got up and gushed about the newlyweds when they were little kids. An objective observer might have forgiven anyone who left early.

After the wedding, Janice went to work in an advertising agency and Tim began work on his CPA. Three years later, Tim was in his first job as an associate at an accounting firm and Janice retired from the ad agency. She dabbled in a dance club for a while and then she became fascinated with antiques, and then, finally, she decided that it was children that would make her life complete.

"I'm not ready for children," Tim said.

"Why not?"

"I'm working fifteen hours a day and trying to make a name for myself, and I need you to be there to back me up, not wiping snot off the face of an infant," he said.

"Well, that doesn't leave much for me to do, does it?" She said.

"You can do anything you want. You just can't be a nursemaid," he said.

Bad blood developed between the two over this, and things did not get better three years later when Tim went into a partnership and started his own firm. Brannigan and James, Financial Advisors and Accountants. But almost immediately, Tim made three times as much money and the sky seemed to be the proverbial limit. He was happy.

"Look Janice, he said one day, things are going great for us and I think it's time we bought a new house. A big one," he said.

"Does that mean that you're ready for children now?" She said.

"After we get the house and we pay off these big insurance policies I've got, then I'll be ready."

"What big insurance policies?" She asked.

"I'm a key man in the business, and so it is part of our partnership agreement that I'll help to pay for a million dollar key man policy. If I die, you get a million dollars and in exchange, you release your interest in my part of the business. Standard stuff."

"And we have to buy this?"

"I have to help the business pay for it, and since we're buying that, I have a chance to buy an additional two million in life coverage for half of what it would usually cost. We have to buy that. That's my advice to us as a financial advisor."

"How long will it take to pay all this stuff off?" She asked, trying to disguise her impatience.

"Probably not more than a year, at the rate we're going," he said. "We should have the insurance paid for and the down payment on the house by then."

Two years after that, they were in the new house, but the children had not yet arrived. The insurance premiums were higher than expected and Tim was working as many hours in his own firm as he had when he first started as an associate. Janice was unhappy. She never got to see her husband and she had no children. She sat alone in the big house, did crossword puzzles and went to the mall.

Janice seemed to be reverting to her pre-Tim days in college. She was listless and had no direction. She also had no interests and nothing to talk about. Gradually, Tim seemed to work later and later. In fact, Tim almost never even came home for dinner any more and often he didn't get home until two or three o'clock in the morning. He would be up by nine and out the door by ten, and she wouldn't see him again until the next morning as he walked past her on his way to the car.

She began to wonder if he was having an affair. He seemed to have less and less interest in her. He had nothing to say to her. She still loved him, she thought, but really, it was beginning to be hard to even remember much about what he was truly like. She watched him sleeping sometimes in the morning, and it was around these times that she built her image of who he was. He was her husband, at home in bed, exhausted from working too many hours.

One morning, she said, "Tim, you've got to do something else with your schedule. I never see you. I don't even know who you are. You don't talk when you're home, and you're never home."

"Jesus, Janice," he said, "What do you want from me? I'm doing what I can. It's not easy to keep up with a new business that's growing."

"What good is it to have a new business that's growing if the rest of your life turns to shit?" She said, with tears in her eyes.

"If you can't find something to do with yourself other than beating on me all the time, maybe you should get some help," he said.

"I'm not beating on you, Tim; I just want you to be a husband to me."

"It's probably the goddam children thing again, isn't it?" He scowled.

"What's wrong with that? What's so wrong with wanting children? I thought you wanted them too," she said.

CHAPTER THREE

In the eighteen months that followed, Tim and Janice argued again and again about having children. She began to get sullen and he nagged at her for her inability to be interested in anything except children. She still loved him, but he was not the man she thought she had married. For one thing, he didn't seem to want children ever, and for another, he wasn't at all supportive of her. Recently, he even seemed to dislike her. Maybe he was right, she thought, and she began to dislike herself.

After almost ten years of marriage, Janice took an assessment of herself. When she got married, she was fifteen pounds lighter and she didn't have bags under her eyes. Now, one of the reasons she didn't socialize with other women she knew was that she was ashamed of the way she looked. She sometimes looked haggard. Tim told her she was still attractive, and sometimes she even believed him, because she could see something of her younger self in the mirror. Her reddish brown hair was cut short, just below the ears, and her brown eyes seemed to compliment her hair. Although her features had always been sharp, especially her nose and her chin, there was also a softness, a feminine quality about her face that seemed to round off the sharpness of her profile.

Fundamentally, she realized, it was not her body that was unattractive. It was her mind. She was in a funk.

Late in the same morning that Tim's car fell into the Monongahela River, Janice was reading the paper, distracted, sitting in her suburban kitchen in the house they had bought south of Pittsburgh in a development called South Pointe. Tim had not come home last night. She was worried and unsure of what to do.

The houses were big, oversized, with six bedrooms, a three car garage, a TV room, a game room, a living room and bathrooms in all unoccupied spaces. The kitchen, though, was bright with good exposure to the morning sun and it had a little alcove area where Janice had put an easy chair and a small TV. It overlooked the large living room that was sunk one step below the kitchen.

Janice and Tim's house was one of three large houses in the entire subdivision that was occupied. Most were still being built or planned and the subdivision was dotted with weed-filled lots or concrete slabs with two by four framing. Janice and Tim's house was the only finished house on their street, although framing had begun across the street and next door. The closest occupied house was half a mile away.

Janice called Tim's office at nine o'clock when it opened, but Tim was not there. No one knew where he was. That threw her into a panic. What could have happened? Tim often worked late, but he was always there in the morning. She filled her coffee cup for the third time and absently settled back in the easy chair, grimacing a little against the glare of the sun and watching as the local news showed pictures of the wreckage of the Liberty Bridge. It seems that it had collapsed last night. No one was injured, miraculously. No cause of the bridge's collapse was known. Officials had ruled out sabotage and there were no explosions. Steel girders that had once supported the bridge were twisted and jutted out where pavement once had been. It looked like an earthquake had struck. Janice watched half-heartedly, uninterested, distracted. Where was Tim?

By three thirty that afternoon, Janice had called Tim's accounting firm a dozen times. No one knew where he was. No one had heard from him. She had decided to call the police when the doorbell rang. It was the police.

Two police detectives politely identified themselves. A black male and a white female. They showed her their identifications and asked if they could come in to speak with her. When she was seated in the living room, they told her that Tim's car had been found. It had surfaced near a sandbar next to Neville Island in the Ohio River, not too far from where the Monongahela River joins with the Allegheny to form the Ohio River.

Janice gasped for air, panic flashed through her. Tears streamed down her cheeks. She sat immobile, stricken. The male detective got her some water; the female detective sat next to her on the couch. Finally, Janice turned and cried on the female detective's shoulder, shocked, scared, but unable to comprehend. How could this be? Tim was just here yesterday. She made him coffee. He kissed her. Maybe there was a mistake, but it was his car. They were telling her that Tim was gone. Killed when his car went off the bridge.

CHAPTER FOUR

Buffalo Gerty's Café was in Pittsburgh's strip district. The sign outside said "No TV but a fight every night." This was an exaggeration, but not by much. On a midweek evening, Jimmy Reynolds sat sipping a beer. He was a construction worker. In fact, he was a construction inspector, working for the contractor who repaired the Liberty Bridge. For three days after the bridge collapse, Reynolds had seen the footage over and over again of the wrecked and fallen bridge. It was not until yesterday, however, that it was released that someone had died. The early reports were that there were no injuries or fatalities. Now it seemed there was a fatality. A car was found down the river, washed up on a sandbar near Neville Island. The victim was a partner in an accounting firm who worked downtown and was apparently coming home from a late night at the office.

Jimmy sipped the beer. Suddenly, the coverage switched from the mangled bridge to reporters chasing a woman across a lawn to a cab. It was the wife of the dead accountant. Her name was Janice Brannigan. Apparently the reporters had been waiting for her outside her house. When she appeared, she was wearing a scarf and dark glasses so that you could not see her face. She ran for the cab, but they caught her as she fumbled to open the door. It was like a football game. She ran, they intercepted and there was a constant commentary on what was happening. She could not manage the door. Her sunglasses fell off and she winced as she stared at the camera, blinded by the camera lights, disoriented, tears running down her face, unable to speak. Reporters shouted questions at her and she just stood. Her mouth moved, but no sound came out. Finally, a female reporter took pity on her and moved in to shield her and to help her with the door. She got in the cab and it pulled off with reporters in close pursuit.

"Jesus," Jimmy said to himself. "That poor woman. How does she feel about the fact that her husband is dead? Could she comment, please, on what it's like to have a loved one drowned in the Monongahela River? Bloodsuckers. There's fuckin lowlifes and then there's fuckin lowlifes."

"What you sayin down there, Jimmy?" Dan, the bartender asked.

Jimmy was thirty-five, medium height and build, neat looking. He'd been a construction worker all his life. His plaid shirt had creases in the sleeves, rolled up two folds; his hair was slightly wavy and brushed back alongside his head; and he was carefully shaved. He looked a little like Clark Gable. A Gerty's regular who looked like a movie star. His masculinity was smooth, well groomed. He hated reporters.

Dan and Jimmy had been friends for years. When Jimmy was still married, the two men and their wives had gone out on the town a number of times. Now and then, Jimmy and Dan played a little softball.

Dan was also a little older that Jimmy. He was a high school jock who dreamed of a career in professional baseball and was still dreaming. He was too short, too square, too muscular in the neck and chest for professional baseball, but he sure could swing a bat.

"You talking to yourself again?" Dan stood in front of Jimmy with an inquisitive look.

"Nah. It's just those fuckin reporters. This woman loses her husband in that bridge collapse and they're all over her wondering whether she's having a good day."

"Yeah, they're regular assholes," Dan agreed, heading off to the cash register.

"Tell me about it," Jimmy said, absently looking at the weather map.

Dan came back. "Hey, weren't you working on that bridge repair job?"

"Yeah. I was."

"What the fuck happened?" Dan said, wiping a glass.

"Beats me, Dan. I gotta go. See you tomorrow." Jimmy slid off the stool, waved and headed for the door.

"Take care, Jim."

Outside, Jimmy stood in the cool night air thinking about being alive instead of dead, about being here on the street instead of under the water. And he thought about that poor woman's face. She couldn't even talk. She couldn't open the car door. Her husband was killed because of the work he did on that bridge. He let them get away with it. If he hadn't, they would have fired him. So he did. He just stood there while they cut corners.

Jimmy told them cutting back on the concrete wouldn't fly and it didn't. That job had disaster written under it, over it and through it, and he had signed off on it. His head hurt and he wanted to go home, get in bed and forget all of this. "It isn't every day that the river kills a girl's husband. Will you be dating now? This must be a really special day for you."

At home Jimmy couldn't sleep. He found himself pacing around the apartment. He stared out windows, studied the contents of the refrigerator, tried to watch TV. Nothing worked. He lay on the couch staring at the ceiling and then, about midnight, he found himself dialing the phone. Information for Timothy Brannigan. No. The residence.

She picked up on the fourth ring. She sounded sleepy.

"Hello?"

"Hello, Mrs. Brannigan. This isn't a crank call. You don't know me, but I saw you this evening on television and I had to call you."

"Who are you?"

"I can't tell you my name, cause if I do, I'll lose my job."

"What do you want?"

"I think I know what happened to that bridge. I think I know why it fell in the water."

"How could you know that? Is this a joke?"

"It's no joke. I worked on the bridge. I saw what they did to it."

"What do you mean?"

"Do you remember from the papers that there was a repair project on the Liberty Bridge?"

"Yes, sort of. I think so."

"Well, I worked on that project and I saw how they repaired the bridge. They didn't do what they were supposed to do."

"I don't believe you. No one would repair a bridge so that it would fall down."

"Mrs. Brannigan, they were supposed to sink two concrete support pillars in the middle of the bridge. Do you remember seeing that on TV?"

"Yes. I think so."

"And they were supposed to run steel beams between the two new pillars and the two old pillars underneath the existing structure. And that was supposed to hold it up."

"I remember something about that. They said it was like a new skeleton for the old bridge."

"That's right. That's what it was supposed to be, but the contractor cheated. He bought smaller, weaker steel and he filled the two new pillars with thick plastic bags of air, so it wouldn't take so much concrete. And that's why the concrete collapsed and the steel didn't hold."

"Why would they do such a thing?"

"Money. They made more money by spending less on materials."

"Oh, my God. They did this?"

"I'm sorry Mrs. Brannigan. I saw you on TV. I felt bad. I can't sleep. I complained to the bosses. I tried to get them to stop. But they wouldn't. They told me to forget it and I knew that if I kept up complaining, they would fire me. I'm sorry. I should have done something. I'm sorry about your husband."

The phone was silent. Jimmy could hear her breathing.

"I'm going to hang up now Mr... ahhh. I don't know your name. I'm going to hang up."

"Wait. Mrs. Brannigan. If you get yourself a lawyer and sue these guys, I'll testify for you. I'll lose my job for sure, but I'll do it. But I won't come forward until you get yourself a lawyer."

"I can't think now. I can't think." She was sobbing.

"If you get a lawyer, leave a message for me at Buffalo Gerty's Café. My name is Jimmy. Give it to the bartender named Dan. Write down your lawyer's number and I will call him. I hope you do it. Those bastards deserve it."

CHAPTER FIVE

Janice worried about the call for almost two weeks. Maybe she should call someone. But why? Would it bring Tim back? Would it make her feel better? Would justice be served? It wouldn't do anything. She would still be alone in that big house. Waiting for a husband who would never come home. It wouldn't help. Besides, she didn't know any lawyers.

But in the second week, the National Casualty and Life Insurance Company called her. An agent wanted to meet with her regarding the key man policy that the firm had on Tim and the individual policies that Tim had on himself.

The insurance man and the partnership's attorney came to her house in the afternoon. The insurance man wore a dark blue suit, polyester blue shirt and a tasteless tie. The attorney wore a gray pinstripe with a white shirt and a red regimental tie. Janice seated them in the living room and the lawyer began.

"I'm here, Mrs. Brannigan, on behalf of your husband's partnership. The business had a policy on your husband's life which, according to the partnership papers, is to be paid to you as payment in full for your husband's interest in the business."

"You are a very fortunate young woman," the insurance man said. "Although your husband's life was insured by my company, his body, as you know, has never been recovered. It is the policy of my company never to pay a life insurance benefit unless there is a corpse. Ahhhhhh, if you'll excuse me for saying so."

"Please, go on," she smiled, wincing inwardly.

"But your husband's accounting firm and their attorney, Mr. Simington here, has convinced my company that it is pointless to wait for a corpse in this case because the Monongahela River, as you know, I'm sure, has a history of not disgorging, ahhhhh, if your excuse me, ahhhhh, its dead. You may remember that in World War II an entire B17 bomber sank in the river and was never found. In light of this and at the insistence of your husband's company lawyer, my company has decided to pay the policy in full."

"I see," Janice said, wishing she were somewhere else.

"Yes, and I'm sure your husband — your late husband — told you that the policies together totaled three million dollars," the insurance man said.

"Yes," she said, suddenly very tired.

The insurance man handed Janice two checks. One for one million dollars, the key man policy for the partnership, and one for two million dollars, the private life insurance policy carried by the insured but also paid for through the business. Janice studied the checks and found herself mindlessly counting the zeros. How many zeros does a million dollars have? She couldn't remember.

"Now, if you'll just sign these papers," the lawyer said, "we'll be through. The one paper releases all of your interest in the partnership in exchange for one million dollars, and the other simply acknowledges that you have received checks totaling three million dollars."

Janice signed both papers and the insurance man handed Janice the checks. In a daze, she showed the men to the door and then came back and stared at the checks. She had been too numb to worry about how she was going to pay the bills, but these checks seemed to answer that question.

* * *

The next morning Janice called her husband's partner and asked him to refer her to a financial adviser. He referred her to a young lawyer that the firm sometimes used who seemed to be quite sharp and would be able to advise her on how to keep her money safe. His name was Roth. She made an appointment with Mr. Roth for later in the week.

* * *

By the time Janice got to Roth's office, two days later, she felt as if she had been anesthetized. She had to do something with all of this money, but the money itself meant nothing to her. It was just a job she had to do. It was like paying the light bill or figuring out your property taxes. It was just something she had to do.

A red-haired, punk-rock secretary showed Janice into Roth's small inner office. The secretary teetered on heels that were too high and led Janice directly to Roth's door. Roth rose from the desk and walked around to shake her hand and introduce himself. He was just under five feet tall and slender. He wore a crisp white shirt and yellow suspenders. His smile was broad, however, and he made Janice feel comfortable. At five-four, Janice towered over him.

Roth gave Janice a number of ideas about how to invest her money and offered to research some of the possibilities that he wasn't current on. They were agreed, however, that she should put at least $750,000 in an annuity that would always be there as an income source, and they would invest the rest, probably in mutual equity and bond funds. Janice wrote him a check to cover the initial deposit into the annuity he recommended.

She was about to leave when Roth asked her if she needed any advice about closing her husband's affairs.

"I think I've got it under control," she said, "Except, of course, the whole thing about why the bridge collapsed."

"You mean you've considered suing PennDOT or the contractor who repaired the bridge?" Roth asked her.

"Well, I didn't really think about it. But last week a man called me up in the middle of the night and said that he knew why the bridge fell down. He said he worked on the bridge, and the contractor didn't put the right materials into the repair."

Roth was jotting notes. "What's this man's name?" he said.

"He only gave me his first name, Jimmy, and said I could reach him at a place called Buffalo Gerty's through a bartender named Dan," she said. "But he promised that if I got a lawyer and sued the contractor, he would testify for me."

"Why would he do that?"

"Because he felt sorry that my husband had been killed. At least that's what he said. It was pretty upsetting."

"If it's true that the contractor used improper materials," Roth said, "You would have a good chance of winning a large sum of money."

"I don't really need money now," Janice said.

"Well, the purpose of a lawsuit like this is partially to punish the person who caused the injury, and not only to benefit the plaintiff," Roth said.

"Punish?"

"Yes. If cheating on the way you do road and bridge repairs gets too costly, people won't cheat. It wouldn't be worth it," Roth said.

CHAPTER SIX

For days Janice fretted about the lawsuit Roth had mentioned. Maybe it was her duty. Maybe Tim would want that. Maybe the contractors would stop killing people if they had to pay for it. Certainly, her life wouldn't be in ruins now if the contractors had not built the bridge the wrong way.

This went on for almost three weeks until, unable to sleep, Janice watched a television program late at night on Mother Teresa. Mother Teresa was a selfless and yet stern advocate for the poor and the sick. Her life was a triumph. She was a model of courage. And then Janice saw an opportunity to be like Mother Teresa. She too could show stern but compassionate resolve. She would sue and she would use the money to help people in need. Maybe she could help children. Maybe she could be around children like Mother Teresa had been. It would be worth a try. Anything was better than sitting endlessly around an empty house.

The next day, Janice told Roth that she would proceed with the lawsuit. Roth went to Buffalo Gerty's Café that evening, and surveyed the area with some trepidation before he got out of his car. People in bandannas, leather jackets, work clothes and just outright bums seemed to frequent Buffalo Gerty's. And then there was the name itself. Who would go to a place called "Buffalo Gerty's Café"?

Nonetheless, after getting worried that he might be mugged in the car, Roth walked into the front door of Buffalo Gerty's . The bouncer waved him in and he approached the bar, in between a man with a pony tail wearing a sleeveless muscle shirt and another man wearing a bandanna and a leather jacket with "Hounds of Hell" embroidered on the back. A group called the "Worthless Momas" was blaring something akin to music on a stage.

"What can I gettcha?" Dan asked, wiping a glass and leaning forward so that he wouldn't have to yell over the music.

"I need to talk to Dan," Roth said.

"I'm him," Dan said, chewing his gum.

"I'm Attorney Roth," Roth said, "And I'd like to leave my card for a man named Jimmy who frequents this place."

"I know Jimmy," Dan said, continuing to wipe the glass.

Roth handed him the card and said, "Thanks."

"You want a drink?" Dan said.

"Ahhh, ahhh, No thanks," Roth said. "Some other time."

The Worthless Mommas belted out, "Dontcha come back no more, no more, no more, no more. Dontcha come back no more."

A few days later Jim Reynolds called Roth in his office and arranged to stop in to see him after work. Reynolds, it turned out, was a construction inspector employed by Badersault Construction Company, the company doing repairs on the bridge. That's how he knew about the irregularities in the repair work. His job was to climb all over the Liberty Bridge project and inspect the work that was being done.

Roth got Reynold's affidavit describing the method by which Badersault defrauded PennDOT and killed Timothy Brannigan. As Reynolds described it, Badersault filled the two new concrete peers half full of inflated plastic blocks. This cut the volume of concrete used by almost forty percent. And they utilized inferior grade steel fastened with inferior welds and substandard rivets. On top of that, they falsified the volume and weight of each load of concrete. Reynolds estimated that Badersault saved approximately one million dollars on materials by doing this. Additionally, Badersault was paid four million dollars to perform the contract.

All of this was possible, Roth explained, because Badersault paid off PennDOT officials with cash, trips and gifts. One day, in the midst of construction, a Badersault van filled with athletic clothes pulled up to the superintendent's trailer. The van was loaded with work out suits, sweat shirts, pants, jackets, raingear. All day long, PennDOT officials pulled up alongside, selected armloads of clothing, and filled up entire back seats with their selections. Rumor had it that there were other gifts too that were not seen, such as tickets to the ball games and golf outings for PennDOT managers, but Reynolds could allege in the lawsuit only what he had seen for himself.

At the time Reynolds gave his affidavit to Roth, he was still employed by Badersault, but he knew his days there were numbered. He had a little time, though, because Roth told him that it would be several months before he would have to divulge Reynolds' name to the opposing side as a witness. Reynolds began quietly looking for other work. In the meantime, Roth filed the lawsuit.

On the day the complaint was delivered all hell broke loose in the Badersault construction site trailers. The company was still on location at the Liberty Bridge, waiting for another government contract to clean up the wreckage and presumably waiting for yet a third contract to rebuild the bridge.

Jim Reynolds was sitting outside the superintendent's trailer when the envelope containing the complaint was opened. The yelling, cursing, shouting and general mayhem inside the trailer could be heard for a block in any direction. Reynolds even imagined that the phone lines draped into the trailer turned red. But if the phone lines weren't actually red, the faces of the men who came out of that trailer were. The entire management team left in three cars and the job site was leaderless. Reynolds decided to have some coffee and eat his sandwich.

A week later, things seemed to be back to normal, but there was a noticeable absence of PennDOT officials on the job site. Inspectors were given make-work jobs inspecting jack hammers and latches on trucks. Work was at a standstill until engineers had decided how to clean things up.

During that week, Reynolds was outside the superintendent's trailer inspecting hoses on air compressors. As he did so, he noticed two strange men going in the superintendent's trailer. One man was black with shiny skin that seemed to be folded in rolls on his face. His black hair was cropped and he was a muscular six feet. He walked like a body builder, though he was in his late forties. His companion was even bigger, over six feet and was straining the seams of a fifty inch shirt. His head seemed a little deformed, flaring out at the top, almost like a mushroom. Maybe it was just the flattop hair style, Reynolds mused.

CHAPTER SEVEN

Oregon Wysorek, Badersault's superintendent of construction for the Liberty Bridge job, sat behind his makeshift plywood desk in the trailer at the construction site. His boss, Wolfgang Badersault, sat in the only overstuffed chair, a chair reserved for him alone during his periodic visits. Wysorek was obese. His belly was so large that even when it was jammed up against the edge of the plywood desk, he had trouble reaching the flat surface of the desk. Sometimes Badersault imagined putting a warning sign on Wysorek's belly that there was imminent danger of explosion. His shirt looked as if several watermelons had been stuffed inside Wysorek's sixty inch waistband.

"Why don't you just send the nigger and Federman? Wax her right there in her house and..." Wysorek said. "The nigger" was Bartholmew Morengeone, a psychopathic killer that Badersault had employed for many years. Federman was his assistant.

"Orey, you're dumb," Badersault said. "You can kill a lawyer without anyone caring. Everybody hates lawyers and lots of people want to kill them. But if you kill the woman, the one who just lost her husband and just filed a lawsuit against yours truly, don't you suppose they'll be looking at me?"

"Yes, sir. I didn't think," Wysorek said.

"You push her, but you don't kill her," Badersault said. "Send her stuff through the mail. Get her scared. But that's all, you understand? "

"O.K. Mr. Badersault."

Wolfgang Badersault, a.k.a. Von Badersault, was a simple crook masquerading as a complex hoodlum. Early in his career as a road builder, he had stumbled on the gold mine widely known as the government contract. At first, he just padded the bill and no one was aware. Then, as the padding increased with each passing year, the bill was padded to the extent that people noticed. But that was quickly remedied by slipping some money to the people who were paying attention.

As time went on, Badersault was known within the Pennsylvania Department of Transportation, the agency in charge of road building, as a force to be reckoned with and symbiotic relationships between PennDot managers,

Badersault and many state legislators were well established. The bottom line was that if Badersault wanted a given PennDot contract, he got it.

But in his middle age, Badersault was tiring of the game. He had scammed every city, county, state and federal agency he had come in contact with and made millions doing it. He had paid off lowly road inspectors and governors and he never performed a government contract in which the state got what it paid for.

In addition to his exploits with state and federal governments, Badersault had also corrupted every human institution remotely connected to road building. When a local truck dealer would not give him favorable terms on a fleet purchase, he had the dealer's trucks banned from any road project in Pennsylvania. The dealer gave in and Badersault got what he wanted. When union leaders wanted to unionize Badersault's company, he took them out to lavish dinners and offered them brown paper envelopes. The need for unions suddenly became less apparent than it had been. Moreover, he raped and pillaged financial institutions for decades, usually simply by taking millions of dollars in interest free loans and either defaulting completely or paying back the loan after he had made a bundle investing the proceeds.

Much to Badersault's amazement, no one objected to any of his chicanery and now he was at the point where it no longer interested him. It was getting boring. In fact, he had turned over daily operation of the business to people like Wesorek. The problem was that Wesorek and others like him were not bright, and Badersault constantly found the need to get involved again to get things back on track.

Badersault had always thought of himself as an aristocrat, and the fact that he was able to cheat his way into the state and federal treasury only solidified his notion that he was royalty. In some circles, he was known alternatively as "The Count" or "Your Honor" and references were made to his Prussian aristocratic lineage. His house, Badersault Hall, was festooned with coats of arms, medieval weapons, suits of armor and colorful flags of the sort used at English county fairs or jousting contests. The house was three stories tall in some sections and four in others. It was made of field stones and vaguely resembled a castle, albeit a jerry-rigged one, since rooms, wings and additions had been put up over the years in a disharmonious conglomeration. There were twenty-one bedrooms, which was reminiscent of the twenty-one gun salute which Badersault imagined appropriate when he left or returned to the estate.

Badersault was much beloved by the poltroons who dotted the county and state political landscape and who came to feed at the Badersault trough. The sheriff, for example, was a dedicated Badersault supporter and regularly sent prisoners to work on the estate, including workers to polish his extensive antique car collection.

Needless to say, the trough was wide and accommodated much larger feeders than the sheriff. Governors, Attorneys General, congressmen, senators and judges were all seen with their chins in the slurry on various occasions.

Badersault watched all of this with a sort of quiet disgust. Even he began to see it as ugly. He began to wonder if the ugliness of his life was affecting him physically. He too was getting ugly. His widely spaced gray eyes were cold, expressionless, unattractive. His cheeks were puffed up, almost swollen with decades of excess food. His mouth was wide and too large with bulbous lips, as if it were left over from an earlier time when such a large mouth was required to feed on all the government contracts he got.

When Badersault was younger, he could eat whatever he wanted and drink himself to stupor every night of the week, then get up, scheme and bribe and do it all over again. Now, he was somewhat frail as a result of stomach stapling surgery he'd had a year ago. His recovery was less than satisfactory.

Two years ago, he had weighed almost four hundred pounds, but today he was a hundred fifty. Every time he ate more than half a sandwich, he threw it up. His weight was dropping and there seemed to be no end to it. His body was bones, organs and slack skin. In fact, his head seemed too big for his body. He'd had two surgeries to remove the stretched-out skin from his chest, arms and legs, but his body still looked like it was draped with thin waves of rubber.

As for friends, he had none. Everyone was interested in his money, that was for sure. But no one was interested in him. About the only thing he could do with people was manipulate them. He was good at that. And it was easy. You just paid them or implied that you would pay them and they did whatever you asked. It was pathetic. But it was also tiring and boring. Continuing to do this no longer interested him. In fact, nothing interested him. He was in a funk.

Badersault was pensive as he sat in the construction trailer in his overstuffed chair. Wysorek knew better than to talk when the boss looked pensive.

"Tell you what, Orey, what we need here is some communication. Call up Bartholmew Morengeone for me and have him go on over to that lawyer's place. You know, the bitch's lawyer. The one's suing us. Tell him to be nice, cool it," Badersault said. "But if the lawyer doesn't want to listen to reason, then persuade him to change his mind."

CHAPTER EIGHT

Bartholmew Morengeone was a free-lance thug who was on retainer for Badersault. He was always available to for whatever violence Badersault required.

It was not uncommon for Bartholmew Morengeone to go for weeks or even months without hearing from Badersault, but when he called, Morengeone and Federman, Morengeone's constant companion, were available.

The two were a formidable force. Federman was of indeterminate age and roughly the size of a refrigerator with a head the shape of a breadbox. Bartholmew Morengeone was black, six feet tall and muscular with a face that was dark, oily and covered with folds of skin, something like a Pug. They were ruthless killers.

Morengeone and Federman came to Badersault's notice a few years earlier when they were working for a labor union that objected to the fact that the port-o-johns on one of Badersault's construction sites were delivered by non-union labor.

In an early attempt to correct the situation, the union sent Bartholmew Morengeone to visit Wysorek, asking him to terminate the non-union deliveries.

"It's not that we object to them non-union shitters," Morengeone said, "But we just think y'all be better off with union shitters. Ya know what I'm sayin?"

"Get the fuck out," Wysorek said. "We ain't gettin no union shitters."

"That be a mistake, Wimbeldon," Morengeone said.

"It's Wysorek," Wysorek said.

"Whatever," Morengeone said.

"Get the fuck out of here," Wysorek said.

"I be back, Wimpie. Don't forget. You had your chance to shit on the fair and square. But no, you wanna shit on the cheap. You gonna be one sorry motherfucker, that's all I can tell yunz."

A week later, Morengeone, Federman and a dozen other thugs showed up at the construction site. They commandeered the heavy equipment, rounded up the two foremen and locked them in separate port-o-johns. Then they took the crane that reached up twenty stories and hoisted both of the occupied port-o-johns as high as they would go, swaying in the air with the foremen screaming to be let out.

Then they muscled Wysorek out of his trailer and taped him to an office chair under the suspended port-o-johns. He fumed and threatened and demanded to be let loose. Morengeone just laughed and told the crane operator to lower the port-o-johns to the fifth floor.

Morengeone gave the obese Wysorek one more chance to agree to union delivery, but he refused and threatened to see Morengeone hung from a tree.

As the thugs melted into the city streets surrounding the construction site, Morengeone and Federman stood at the gate to the site and detonated a small explosive in each of the port-o-johns that blew the floors out and emptied fifty gallons of excrement and toilet paper on Wysorek.

It also left both foremen hanging by their fingers to keep from falling out of the blown-out port-o-johns. Crane operators ran to lower them down and other laborers approached Wysorek reluctantly to get him untaped from the chair.

As they worked on the tape, the two port-o-johns were being lowered and one of the foremen lost his grip, falling from a distance of fifteen feet and knocking Wysorek, still taped to the chair, to the ground into the puddled excrement.

Badersault arrived at the scene just as the port-o-johns blew up. He was bent over laughing as Wysorek took the shit bath and then as foreman knocked him into the puddles.

Within a few days, the deliveries were being made by union laborers and Bartholmew Morengeone and Federman were on Bartholomew's retainer.

CHAPTER NINE

The girl behind the desk was dumpy. She was twenty-five years old with a round face topped with a metallic red mop. She looked at the two men in front of her as if they were visitors from another planet and she was not far wrong.

"Do you have an appointment?" She said.

"I don't make appointments," the tall, muscular black man said. His face was covered with folds of skin that were shiny and prickly with stubble. He looked as if he were sweating, but it was too cool for that.

The black man's companion stood behind him, silent, larger, taller, white. His head was square. He had grown out of his size 50 jackets.

"I'm not sure Mr. Roth can see you right now," she said.

"Why don't you ask him," the black man said, grinning so that two enormous yellow canine teeth flashed out at her.

"Who should I say is here to see him?" She asked.

"Morengeone," he said. "And Federman."

"Morengeone?" She mouthed, quietly, screwing up her mouth in a gesture of comedy.

"Morengeone," he said, coolly, his bloodshot eyes boring into the girl's eyes.

A fear that her brain was being seared by Morengeone's eyes propelled her out of her chair and down the hall to Roth's office. She knocked and went in. Shortly she came out and said nervously, "Mr. Roth will see you, but he only has a few minutes before he has to leave for court."

The two large men went into Roth's office. Roth was standing behind his desk when they entered. He was a little under five feet tall and thin. Next to his visitors, he appeared fragile.

"Hello, I'm Dave Roth," he said, motioning to chairs in front of his desk.

"I'm Morengeone," the black man said, grinning, with the yellow canines showing. "And this," pointing to his companion, "is Federman."

"Mr. Morengeone, Mr. Federman, pleased to meet you," Roth said, coming around the desk and extending his hand. "I only have a minute, as my secretary mentioned, before I have to leave for court. I have a jury trial starting today."

Morengeone grinned a toothy smile and took the hand, squeezing it as if it were chick in the jaws of a fox. Roth involuntarily let out a yelp and the secretary came clattering in, wobbling on her high heels, her face at the door, fearful. Morengeone released the hand.

"It's all right Debbie," Roth said, his face bright red, tears threatening to spill over the edges of his eye sockets, holding his injured hand with the other hand.

Roth retreated behind his desk, rubbing the hand. All thoughts of the jury trial were suddenly gone, replaced by a fear of the men sitting in front of his desk. Morengeone smiled his canine smile. Roth couldn't imagine what these thugs were after. Maybe they needed a lawyer. They probably did. Just wanted to show him who was boss, but Jesus, his hand might never work again.

"What can I do for you gentlemen?" Roth said with as much control as he could muster.

"We'd like you to tell Janice Brannigan to knock it off," Morengeone said.

"I'm sorry?" Roth said, leaning forward as if he were hard of hearing.

"Just tell the bitch to get the fuck out 'a the lawsuit," the black man said.

"The bitch?"

"Yeah, Brannigan. The bitch."

Roth's reaction was as unthinking as a kneejerk. He was fanatic about his clients' privacy and about his zealous representation of them. "I can't discuss the business of my clients with you," Roth said, incredulous, as he continued to massage his hand.

"That's too bad," Morengeone said, "Cause if you don't tell her to get the fuck out of the lawsuit, she's gonna get hurt and so are you."

"I think you both should leave," Roth said. As he heard himself say these words, he realized he had made a mistake. He needed to tell them what they wanted to hear, but it was too late for that and he realized his body was turning cold with fear.

"You ain't listening." Morengeone said. "He ain't listening, is he Federman?"

The big white man shook his head no.

"Federman thinks you ain't listening, and when people don't listen, they get hurt," Morengeone said. "You coulda just tol the bitch to chill out and we coulda jus walked outa here. But no, you gotta fuck wit me. So now I gotta fuck wit you."

"I don't want any trouble from you gentlemen," Roth said. "Please just leave. No trouble."

Federman lunged across the desk and grabbed Roth by the shirt, then hauled him over the desk, lifting him into the air with one arm, his body knocking things over and dragging papers off the top of the desk. The glass in a picture frame shattered as the frame hit the floor.

Roth's feet were kicking in the air and he had both hands wrapped around Federman's huge hand, trying to get loose. His mouth opened and closed and he made a slight gurgling sound. Federman carried him into the outer office, his feet sometimes dragging, sometimes in mid-air as they moved toward the door. Occasionally, Roth's struggling would throw Federman off balance and Federman would bounce him off the wall or into a chair. Morengeone was behind him.

The red haired secretary stood at her desk with her hand to her mouth and her other hand on the telephone. Morengeone smiled at her and quick-stepped over, hitting her with a cross that broke her jaw and sent her sprawling against the wall, unconscious. Morengeone picked up the telephone, put it back on the girl's desk and walked out the door.

Federman carried Roth outside, his feet dangling and kicking, and opened the door of a mini van. There was a thud as Roth's body bounced off the floor of the minivan. Federman climbed in after him, pushed Roth's body flat on the floor in front of a captain's chair where he sat and put his foot on Roth's face. Roth gurgled, but he didn't move.

Morengeone went back into Roth's office and shuffled through the files on his desk. The Badersault file had been knocked to the floor. It was fairly thick. Morengeone picked it up and went outside to the truck. He got in the driver's side and drove off.

In twenty minutes they arrived at a concrete plant near the Monongahela River under the Brady Street Bridge. It was a Badersault plant. They pulled into a covered area next to a big concrete truck. A ladder had been placed against the truck leading up to the opening of the hopper that held seven cubic yards of concrete mix.

Federman got out of the mini van, reached in and dragged the terrified Roth out and onto the ground. Roth was whimpering and begging Federman not to hurt him. He looked around desperately for help. They were in a concrete plant. There must be workmen around. Roth's head swiveled furiously and Federman lifted him off the ground and then off his feet again, but this time, he was dangling in mid air as Federman climbed the ladder and Roth struggled, kicking his feet.

When Federman got to the top, he struggled a little, and then using both arms, he lifted the kicking Roth into the opening of the truck's concrete hopper. Roth, still outside the hole in the hopper, resisted, bracing both arms against the edges of the hole he was looking into. Federman pulled the kicking, struggling Roth over to him and, shifting the load to one hand, hit him a stunning blow with the other. Roth went limp.

Federman then, using both hands, stuffed him into the hole on the top of the hopper. First his head, with his body bent double outside the hopper, then, grabbing Roth by his ass, he pushed him in and they heard a slight thunk as Roth hit bottom. Federman climbed down from the ladder and a workman who had been smoking nearby got in the cab of the truck and drove fifty yards to a device that poured in gravel, cement and water in sufficient quantities to make six cubic yards of concrete. Within fifteen minutes, the truck left the plant, weighed and logged out, the hopper turning with the sound of gravel being mixed with cement.

Three days later, a cement encrusted Roth was pulled out of the Monongahela River near the Point in downtown Pittsburgh. The cement had given him third degree burns over a hundred percent of his body. He died of suffocation.

* * *

At about the same time the harbor police were pulling Roth's body out of the water near Point State Park, Morengeone and Federman were meeting half a mile away in the superintendent's trailer at the Liberty Bridge construction site with Oregon Wysorek.

Morengeone sat in a wooden arm chair opposite Wysorek's desk, tilted back on two legs with his feet on the desk. His malevolent bloodshot eyes stared at Wysorek, who was leafing through the file stolen from Attorney Roth's office.

Wysorek's fingers were pudgy, like his face and his whole fat body. His jowls wobbled as he swung his face from the left page to the right. A gaudy ring glimmered on a thick finger. His eyes seemed engulfed in swollen puffs of skin.

"The only name in this file," Wysorek said, "Is Jimmy Reynolds. He works for us. He's an inspector."

"I guess that's how they knew what kind of a scam you wuz running. What wit them fake bills for the concrete and shit like that," Morengeone said.

Wysorek glared at him. "Mr. Badersault is gonna be livid. I can't believe they know all this stuff," he said, the jowls shaking.

"Yeah, well, they die just like everybody else," Morengeone said.

Wysorek looked at him. Morengeone shrugged. "You're right," Wysorek said. "They do die like everybody else."

CHAPTER TEN

For the next two weeks, Wysorek sent Janice threats. The usual stuff: "Don't do this." "Be careful." "Watch your back." "We know where you live." He even called her from pay phones several times with vague threats. Janice was scared out of her mind. She called her lawyer but his office seemed to be closed.

When the threats kept coming and she couldn't reach her lawyer, Janice began to fall apart. She didn't know who to turn to. She knew the police would be useless. Finally, she screwed up her courage and called her husband's college friend, Richard Scuilli. He would know what to do. He was the district attorney.

Scuilli received her call politely and told her he was sorry to hear of Tim's death. When he heard about the threats she had received, he paused, got more details about what they said and then agreed that she needed help.

Scuilli said, "I hate to say this, but the police won't be any help. I think I know someone who can help. He's probably expensive. I know he's effective. If you want, I can try to get in touch with him."

"Please, Richard, I am scared. I've never been so scared."

"Yes, and I think you're right to be concerned."

"I can pay. I inherited some money from Tim. Just tell him I need help."

"Can you stay in your house for two or three days?"

"Yes."

"Don't let anyone in, even a policeman. The only exception is the man I'm going to call. His name is John Donne. You got that?"

When Scuilli hung up with Janice, he thought about what he was doing. He didn't want to see the woman get hurt, and he couldn't go against Badersault directly because Badersault paid the Scuilli political machine too much money. Badersault was a blowhard and impossible to deal with for the most part. He acted like a buyer for Walmart: his way or no way. Then there was that idiotic pretension to aristocracy. What a crock of shit. The guy was a moron.

Besides that, he was unpredictable. If Scuilli went to him, there was no telling what he would do. He might explode at Scuilli's interference and cause all kinds of trouble with Scuilli's uncle Rocco. That was best avoided.

So he placed the ad: "John Donne. Please call. 412-565-5500. Ask for Richard." That was how one got in touch with John Donne, a.k.a. Sam Budda.

The next day John Donne called. "This is John Donne, answering your ad."

"Hello, Sam. This is Richard Scuilli."

There was a silence on the line. Then, "I didn't expect to hear from you," Sam said.

"I have a favor to ask. A guy I went to school with just got killed. His widow is suing the contractor that did the bridge work that killed him. The contractor is upset. Apparently he is threatening to harm her. She's getting threats and she's scared shitless."

"So you immediately think of me. Why not take care of it yourself?"

"Can't. The contractor is a big political contributor. If he thought I went against him, he'd figure he wasn't getting his money's worth."

"Hell, Richard, you don't need any political contributors. You just shoot anyone who votes against you."

"Yeah, I know, but I don't get his contributions. He contributes to our people all over the state. They get the contributions and they're happy. He stops the contributions and they're not happy. Then I have lots of grief."

"Can this lady pay my fee?"

"She says she inherited money from Tim, her husband."

"You're not involved in any way?" Sam said.

"No."

"I'm not going to run into any of your goons?"

"No. I told you. I got nothing to do with it. I'm clear of it. I don't want to touch it or be associated with it. It would be a favor to me if you'd talk to her. That way I don't have to call Badersault and cause all kinds of trouble."

"Who is Badersault?"

"He's the contractor that worked on the bridge. If I had to guess, it fell down because he shorted them on the repairs."

"All right. I appreciate the referral. I'll have a talk with the lady. What's her name?"

"Janice Brannigan. Lives in South Point."

"I'll call her up. Thanks."

"Don't mention it. Remember when we last talked? In the mausoleum? This is how it should work. We get along without killing each other."

Sam hung up. He was still troubled about that conversation. Scuilli was a mobster.

CHAPTER ELEVEN

Two days later, Sam pulled the Landcruiser into the driveway at 1326 Brenmawyr Place, South Point, the residence of Janice Brannigan. The house was the size of a beached battleship and its windows gleamed like portholes in the sun. It reached up four stories and had an integral garage. The yard was large, but unremarkable. A few shrubs dotted the perimeter of the house. No flowers or trees. Pretentious.

A scratching movement came from the back of the truck.

"You stay here, Ronin. Guard the car." The big black head growled quietly. Ronin was a hundred fifty pound Akita.

Sam stepped out of the Landcruiser and clicked the lock as he headed for the house. He wasn't protecting the car from thieves so much as he was protecting the thieves from getting beheaded as they tried to jump the ignition.

Sam's cropped gray hair seemed white in the sun above the tropical weight safari coat he wore over his gun. The gun belt was a Mitch Rosen custom inch and a half, saddle leather, double thickness and it held up both the Baer Thunder Ranch .45 and the tan corduroy pants.

Sam rang the bell and nothing happened. He thought he saw curtains flutter in a window, but he wasn't sure. On the third ring, a small voice inside said, "Who are you?"

"John Donne. I'm here to see Mrs. Brannigan."

The door opened a little and Janice's chiseled features and brown eyes appeared, hiding behind the thick edge of the door. She looked at Sam and said nothing.

"Hi," he said softly. "Are you Mrs. Brannigan?"

"Yes," she replied cautiously, her mouth thin and compressed. "Do you have identification?"

Sam smiled. Any identification she might want to see was as close as the nearest Xerox machine. "Sure," he said, pulling out a wallet with his Pennsylvania private detective license and a business card. She looked at both, handed back the wallet and opened the door.

"Sorry," she said. "I've been scared."

Sam stepped in. The foyer was two stories tall, paved with flagstones and twelve feet square. A huge chandelier, at least four feet in diameter, hung from the ceiling. The living room opened to the left, the dining room to the right, and the kitchen more or less straight ahead. Sam followed the woman into the kitchen. She motioned to a stool and Sam sat at a counter overlooking the living room. Without asking, the woman put a cup of steaming coffee in front of him, poured one for herself, and sat down at the counter. He shifted his stool a little so that he faced her.

The woman was pretty, but tense. Her mouth was a tight, thin line. Her short hair was an auburn brown and a little tousled. She wore jeans, a red sleeveless top and tennis shoes. She sipped her coffee.

"You want to tell me about why I'm here?" Sam said.

She turned to him, almost as if she had forgotten he was there.

"Please excuse me," she said. "Ever since Tim ..."

And there she trailed off. A tear appeared in the corner of the eye closest to Sam. Sam looked into the living room and waited.

"Ever since Tim died," she continued, "I've been a wreck."

"When we talked on the phone, you said something about fearing for your life."

"I'm terrified," she sobbed.

She got off the stool and went to the other side of the kitchen, opened a drawer, pulled out a stack of envelopes and handed them to Sam. The one on top said, "BACK OFF. The one under that arrived today said, "YOU SEE WHAT HAPPENED TO YOUR LAWYER."

"What's this one mean? What happened to your lawyer?" Sam said.

"I don't know what it means. I've been trying to call my lawyer for a week and no one answers."

"That doesn't sound too good," Sam said.

"Do you have any idea who sent these?"

"I assume it's the contractor I sued. Who else would be threatening me?"

"I don't know. Do you or your husband have any enemies or people who want to harm you?"

"No."

Tears welled up again and the woman sipped coffee through her tight lips. She brushed a tear aside with the back of her hand.

Sam sat silently for a minute, reluctant to push too much on the woman's reservoir of fear and grief. After a time, Sam got up from the stool.

"I'm going out to the car," Sam said. He went out the front door. Shortly, Janice heard the door open and turned to see Sam coming back in, holding the leash of a very large dog. His black head, shaped like a bear, was enormous, almost a foot across between the ears.

Ronin was alert. He was in new surroundings and eager to see what was there. Even as Sam turned to close the door, Ronin stood erect, almost at attention, scanning the inside of the house. The huge head had orange, intelligent eyes, and his fur was thick, double layered and colored brown, black and white in a pinto pattern. He was wide at the shoulders and his paws were so big that it looked as if even he could never live up to them. He strained at the leash.

Ronin was an Akita and he was larger than normal for the breed. The Akita is the Japanese national dog and was bred for hunting bear. Some Akitas, including Ronin, have bearlike faces; others are more doglike, with longer muzzles. Akitas have a reputation for extreme loyalty, extreme fierceness and extreme strength.

The most famous Akita, Hachiko, is said to have walked to the train station in Koyoto every day with his master, where the master boarded the train for work. In the afternoon, the dog returned to meet him. On May 21, 1925, Dr. Eisaburo Ueno, Hachiko's owner, died at work. That evening, Hachiko sat among priests and mourners for his master. After that, Hachiko went to the station every morning and again every afternoon to wait for his master. People came to know the dog and cared for him during his vigil. On March 7, 1935, Hachiko was found dead at the spot where he waited for his master every day. The Koyoto train station has a statue of the dog prominently displayed.

Janice's eyes widened at the appearance of the dog. His head looked like a giant teddy bear. She put down her coffee and got off the stool. As Sam walked toward her with Ronin on the leash, Ronin wagged his tail and tugged at the leash to go up to Janice. This was most unusual. Akitas normally stand off to see whether this is an occasion for extreme violence or merely another petting.

"He likes you," Sam said. "Just stand there and let him sniff you for a minute."

Ronin approached Janice and sniffed her legs, then her crotch and she embarrassedly moved back.

"All dogs do that," Sam said. "Don't be nervous. Now let him sniff your hand. Move slowly so he won't be threatened."

Ronin sniffed Janice's hand and his tail wagged again.

"O.K. You can slowly move your hand up and scratch him behind his ears."

Janice scratched Ronin's ears and he looked up at her and danced a little as she scratched him. Then he made a sound a little like a mixture of a growl and a howl. Janice pulled her hand back, afraid.

"That's his way of talking to you," Sam said. "He doesn't normally talk to people he doesn't know. That's good that he's talking to you. If you want to try something else, kneel down facing away from him. If he wants you to keep petting him he will come up to you."

Janice kneeled down and Ronin promptly came up to her side and licked her ear. Then he nuzzled her throat with his wet black nose and almost pushed her over backwards. Janice caught her balance with her hands and faced the big dog on her knees. He came up to her and licked her ear again. She put her arms around his massive neck and sobbed. Her head was almost lost in the immense body of the dog. Janice buried her face in Ronin's furry shoulder and Ronin stood there, nuzzling her hair, periodically looking at Sam.

After a time, Ronin moved away and Janice got to her feet. She wiped her eyes, a little embarrassed.

"Ronin seems to take to you," Sam said. "Let's go in the living room. Sit across the room from me if you would."

Ronin followed Sam into the living room and lay down at his feet. Janice sat across the room in a wingback chair.

"Can you stay in the house for the rest of the day?" Sam said. "I have a meeting scheduled this afternoon. I've asked some of my associates to do some research on Badersault Construction Company. I'd like you to stay here with Ronin. If you can do that, I'll know that you're safe."

"Yes. I can do that. Thank you. I haven't felt safe for a long time."

"Maybe we can fix that," Sam said. "Ronin, Protect."

Ronin looked at Sam, got up and walked across the room toward Janice. He lay down at her feet, put his massive head between his paws and closed his eyes.

"You're protected," Sam said.

Janice looked down at the enormous dog and quietly said, "Thank you," almost whispering.

"It's kind of hard to get past Ronin," Sam said. "But don't open the door for anyone. Ronin knows that his job is to protect you and if someone comes into the house, he may interpret their presence as a threat."

"O.K. I'll keep the door locked."

"You have to understand," Sam said. "Ronin can kill a man, and if he believes you are threatened, that's what he will do. And by the way, I'd like you to close the blinds or curtains of any room you are likely to be in and stay away from windows where you can. If you see someone outside, call the police, then call me and barricade yourself in a room with Ronin. Can you do that?"

"Yes. Our bedroom is on the second floor and it has a door that locks."

"All you have to do is go there. Ronin will follow you wherever you go."

"O.K."

Sam brought in Ronin's food and water bowls and then left for his meeting.

"There's one other thing," Sam said. "I go by the professional name John Donne, but my real name is Sam Budda. You can call me Sam."

She smiled and whispered, "O.K."

As Sam drove away, he thought, "They'll kill her if they're determined. They'll shoot her through a window or set fire to her house and kill her when she runs out. But at least she has a chance now. And they won't kill her at close range. Ronin will see to that."

CHAPTER TWELVE

Carnegie Mellon University is located in the Oakland section of Pittsburgh. It is widely known and respected as being on the cutting edge of all things related to artificial intelligence. The campus is a pleasing mix of old and new architectural styles and sits on the edge of Schenley Park, giving it a somewhat pastoral flavor. One of the buildings, Baker Hall, is a long brick affair of indiscriminate design, stretching three hundred yards down a sloping hill. The hallway inside, concrete and wide, also slopes downward. The story goes that Baker Hall was one of the original buildings and it was designed by the co-founder, Andrew Carnegie. Carnegie's idea was that if the college didn't work out, Baker hall could easily be converted into a gravity fed assembly plant.

Sam's meeting was with his partner, Nick Savarese, and a computer expert who worked at CMU, John Merriweather. When Sam arrived, the two men were seated in an isolated section of the dining room. Nick had a pronounced humped nose, olive skin and a generous mouth. He wore a polo shirt, khakis and a large UTS chronograph on his left arm. The other man was in his forties, of slight build and had no chin. His face came down to his mouth and then trailed off at an angle into his neck. He wore a lightweight summer sport coat and a floppy white shirt with a tie.

Nick saw Sam enter the room and stood to introduce John Merriweather. Sam and Merriweather shook hands and the three sat, Merriweather looking a bit shrunken between the two larger men.

Nick had been referred to Merriweather by an acquaintance in the private investigation business that had used him to break into computers in a high profile case. Merriweather was expensive, but good, and he was a Walter Middy private eye. When Nick explained that they were looking into the possibility that Badersault's defective repair of the Liberty Bridge may have resulted in a man's death, Merriweather could hardly wait to begin.

"John was telling me," Nick said, "That he found some stuff on our target. You tell him, John."

"You asked for everything I could find on Badersault Construction Co. I found the usual stuff, you know, incorporation registration in Delaware, principal place of business in Monroeville, Pa., names of officers and directors, judgments and liens."

"Anything unusual?" Sam asked.

"Not really. A few lawsuits between Badersault as the general contractor and some subs, and a few suits back and forth about defective equipment, but nothing unusual," Merriweather said.

Merriweather continued, "So I went into some protected files to see whether their name or the names of their people came up."

"These, ah, protected files," Sam said. "Am I correct in thinking they are not available to the public?"

"Yes," Merriweather said. "They are encrypted and protected by multiple layers of passwords."

"You can penetrate that?"

"Absolutely. There aren't many systems I cant get into."

"All right," Sam said. "That's good to know."

"Well, I found nothing, even in the FBI files, until I got to the files of United States Attorney in Pittsburgh. There I found a complete file on Badersault. I downloaded the entire thing and I forwarded it to your lawyer, Cochran, yesterday."

"I assume Cochran will be able to explain what that is all about," Sam said. "Anything else?"

"Well yes. Just by accident, I was able to get into the Badersault internal network of computers. Normally, such a network would be absolutely impenetrable because there would be no connection to the outside world, but someone in Badersault's accounting department has a penchant for pornographic web sites, and their access to the web gave me a porthole that I could use to get in. Basically what I found there were two sets of books. I'm no accountant, so I don't really know what this means, but for any given day, they have two sets of books with different income and expenses on that day. I copied all this stuff too and sent it to Cochran."

"Outstanding, John. Has Nick already paid you?"

"Yes, and I thank you both. You are very generous. Thank you."

Sam, rising, said, "Our pleasure, John. We'll be in touch."

As the slim man with no chin shuffled out, Sean Cochran came walking in. Cochran worked out of his one-man law office. He was in his late thirties and had just begun to lose a little hair. His manner was businesslike, but friendly. A bit of a renegade, Cochran liked working with Sam and Nick.

The three men greeted each other and then sat and talked easily as they ordered steak salads, rolls and iced tea.

"So what is the U.S. Attorney doing with a file on our friend Badersault?" Sam asked.

"Someone filed an action against Badersault claiming that Badersault had defrauded the government in the work they did on the Liberty Bridge," Cochran said.

"Why didn't Merriweather find this lawsuit when he did his regular search of the lawsuits that have been filed?" Nick said.

"Because this is a special kind of lawsuit. If you file one of these, it has to go to the U.S. Attorney under seal. That means that it's secret until the U.S. Attorney makes it public by releasing it. The U.S. Attorney looks at it and decides whether he wants to get involved," Cochran said.

"Why is this lawsuit treated differently than any other lawsuit?" Sam said.

"Because it was filed under the False Claims Act. The False Claims Act is a federal statute passed after the Civil War because contractors were rebuilding the South and ripping off the government. They were making false claims for work they never performed. The government sought to prevent that by allowing private citizens to bring these False Claim Act lawsuits and collect part of the proceeds from people who had cheated the government. But some con-artist plaintiffs brought False Claim Act lawsuits even though they had no false claims, and so the government started requiring that these lawsuits be filed under seal to protect innocent defendants from having their reputations ruined."

"O.K.," Sam said, "We have a lawsuit against Badersault alleging that he made false claims against the government. And this lawsuit is secret, under seal, and it was filed before Janice Brannigan's lawsuit. Who brought this lawsuit?"

"Some guy named Blinkman. He works for PennDot. He's claiming Badersault shorted the government on materials for the Liberty Bridge repair."

"How would he know that?" Nick said.

"Apparently he was some kind of government inspector," Cochran said.

"This False Claims Act," Sam said. "What does it allow the plaintiff to recover?"

"That's just it," Cochran said. "It allows for triple damages and attorney's fees. If the plaintiff wins, he gets up to twenty-five percent of the take and attorney fees. A case like this could cost Badersault several million dollars."

"So when does Blinkman's case go to court?" Nick said.

"It doesn't," Cochran said. "The United States Attorney has to approve these lawsuits, and this one wasn't approved. It's done. Blinkman is done."

"Why?"

"Probably because Badersault paid off the U.S. Attorney or one of the U.S. Attorney's bosses," Cochran said.

"So this guy Blinkman knew about problems with the Liberty Bridge a while ago, probably while it was being worked on," Sam said.

"Yes. Blinkman says Badersault bought lighter steel than was called for, didn't use the right size rivets or enough of them, used cheap defective welds and had some kind of a air compressor that forced air into huge plastic balloons inside the new bridge pillars. He claims that the pillars were half filled with air instead of concrete. Then Badersault billed the state for all of the concrete and steel called for in the plans even though he used only a fraction of that amount."

"If Blinkman knew the contractor was shorting the state, why didn't he just stop it?" Sam said.

"He says he tried. He complained to his boss, and the boss blew him off. Then he complained to the big boss and the big boss blew him off too," Cochran said. "He claims they were all paid off by Badersault."

"So this guy Blinkman is in a bad spot now," Nick said.

"Well, he's in a real bad spot because, he's been with PennDOT twenty years and he claims that ever since he filed his False Claims suit, PennDot tried to get him to quit, cut his benefits, gave him a different job, took his office away from him, and didn't allow anyone to talk to him," Cochran said, drinking his tea.

"Is Blinkman still at PennDOT?" Sam said.

"Don't know. As of the filing of the lawsuit, he was," Cochran said. "Oh, and what's your client's lawyer's name? It isn't Roth is it?"

"Yeah, why?" Sam said.

"According to the paper, they just fished him out of the river," Cochran said.

CHAPTER THIRTEEN

On Fridays, Buffalo Gerty's Café had a bouncer. The crowds were heavy. The bouncer sat on a stool by the door. He was a gym rat wearing a wife-beater. As he checked all the young people, he said, "Buffalo Gerty's 's the name; shot and a beer's the game." The girls giggled and their dates guffawed. The dates were manly.

The bar's clientele was a mixture of working stiffs and young professionals who wanted to show that they were working stiffs at heart. At the bar, Jimmy Reynolds sipped a beer. It was Friday night and he was on his third. He watched the crowds of laughing couples and mused. He thought about his ex-wife. People like him came to bars so they wouldn't be lonely. So why was he lonely? Maybe going to bars was like the other things in his life. It didn't work. Now he sat at the bar reading another front page story about the collapse of the Liberty Bridge.

"Weren't you on that Liberty Bridge job?" Dan said.

"Yeah," Jimmy said. "I told 'em about that concrete, but ain't nobody wanting to listen. I told 'em."

A few minutes later, Dan came back with a fist full of dollar bills and stopped long enough to say, "You mean you knew that it was gonna fall down?"

"Well hell no, Dan. I didn't know it was gonna fall down, for Christ's sake. Gimmie another beer, will you? I just knew they weren't using as much concrete as they were supposed to."

Dan came back with change for the other customer and a new beer for Jimmy. "Well, didn't you tell 'em? Wasn't that your job?"

"Hell yes, I told 'em. They didn't wanta hear. They told me not to worry about it."

Dan left to give the other guy his change and pick up some new orders. Finally he came back and said, "Well at least you told 'em."

"It's just the usual contractor shit, Dan. You know, cut corners, buy cheap stuff, bill for expensive stuff, use five and bill for ten. The usual shit," Jimmy mumbled, talking to himself now, as Dan had moved away.

Ten feet down the bar to Jimmy's right, a fight erupted. Dan moved quickly toward the two men, who had each other by the throats and were leaning on the bar trying to kill each other. By the time Dan got there with the ball bat, the bigger man had the back of the smaller man's head on the bar, and the smaller man's eyes were starting to roll back in his head. His grip on the bigger man fell away. In a fluid movement, Dan stepped in and drove a home run right through the big man's shoulder. There was a loud crack as the bat hit home. The big man fell away and the small man slumped to the floor. The gym rat appeared and lifted the big man to his feet. He stood lopsided, nursing a broken shoulder.

"Jesus Christ, you fuck. You broke my shoulder," the big man yelled. That's when the gym rat broke his nose, then led him out to the street, bellowing, cursing, screaming and threatening to murder them all. Dan came around and threw cold water on the smaller man, who shook his head and seemed to regain consciousness.

When Dan came back behind the bar, Jimmy said, "How many times I seen you do that, Dan? You'd think they'd learn."

"Hell, Jim. These guys can't even learn their names right." The gym rat was back at his post at the door and the smaller blonde man was slumped in a booth with a woman in a very short skirt smoothing his hair.

Jimmy looked over and chuckled, "Maybe I should get somebody to choke me like that."

"Might be arranged," a voice next to him said.

In the excitement of the fight and the aftermath, Jimmy had not noticed that someone sat in the seat to his left. Jimmy turned to look.

The new arrival was a black man in his fifties. His thick face was creased with folds of shiny flesh, his close cropped hair was receding, and a heavy stubble was visible on the folded, wrinkly face. His large flat nose had been broken. More than once. As he grinned, huge yellow canine teeth appeared at each side of his mouth. He watched Jimmy watch him. His eyes were bloodshot at the edges.

Jimmy instantly recognized him as the man who had gone into the superintendent's trailer at work some days ago, but he said, "I don't think I know you."

"Probably not," the black man said. "Mr. Badersault asked me to meet with you. Me and my associate," pointing to a man standing behind him. "My name is Bartholomew Morengeone . This is Federman."

Morengeone grinned another grin and the canine teeth made another appearance.

Federman didn't speak. He looked at Jimmy with something like a leering grin.

Jimmy was suddenly alarmed. Nothing good was going to come of this. These two guys looked like a nightmare come to life. Jimmy sat there and considered what his options were, or if he had any. His mind raced between abject helpless fear, as if he had just been thrown into a pit full of poisonous snakes, and insane hope that he could just bound up into the air and fly out of there. While he was mulling over these possibilities, Federman stepped around and grabbed him under the far arm while Morengeone grabbed him under the close arm. Jimmy was too startled to struggle, and they dragged him across the room, his feet sometimes walking and sometimes dragging, to a vacant table along the far wall. Morengeone pushed him into a chair next to the wall and sat next to him while Federman sat across the table from him.

"What the hell do you guys want?" Jimmy stammered, frightened and uncertain of what was going on. He looked around desperately for weapons, but nothing presented itself. There was a napkin holder, a candle and a cardboard advertisement.

Morengeone said, "Mr. Badersault thought you might be having some trouble keeping your mouth shut, and from what I heard tonight, I think he's right."

"Keep my mouth shut," Jimmy said. "About what?"

"About the bridge. What else?" Morengeone said.

"Oh. So that's it," Jimmy said. He was awake and sober now.

"So Federman and me, we'd like you to take a ride wit us. No trouble. Just so we can talk about this. Maybe we can work something out wit you," Morengeone said.

While Morengeone was talking, Jimmy's hand closed on the glass globe about the size of a softball that was filled with wax and a burning wick. Jimmy kept Morengeone occupied by locking his eyes on the bloodshot crazy eyes of his adversary. Federman, Jimmy could see in his peripheral vision was locked on them locking on each other.

All Jimmy could think of was his own mangled body being found on a back road after these two had beaten him to death with sledge hammers.

Even Federman didn't see it coming. Just as Morengeone finished his murderous proposal masked as a friendly chat, Jimmy slammed the glass bowl of fire and hot wax into Morengeone's eyes with all the strength he had. Morengeone bellowed an immediate outraged scream, and seized his own head with both hands, trying to swat the glass and fire and wax from his face and his eyes.

Jimmy jumped from his chair, grabbed it by the back and swung it at Federman. The blow didn't hurt Federman, but it slowed him down long enough for Jimmy to sprint past him toward the bar. He hit the bar with both arms outstretched and vaulted over, overshooting his mark a bit and crashing into a row of bottles lined up in front of the mirror. Federman was right behind him. His arms too were on the bar and he was halfway over, in mid-air, when Dan swung the bat with all the power he had. It hit with a thwack dead center on Federman's forehead and he went down like an anvil dropped from the sky.

"Steeeeeeeeerike," some fool down the bar yelled.

CHAPTER FOURTEEN

Jimmy Reynolds ran out the back door of Buffalo Gerty's with a speed he didn't know he had. He kept looking back, fearing that the nightmares might burst out the back of the bar, catch him and kill him. He nearly collided with a lamp post. Finally, he made it to his truck, beeped the lock release, jumped in and fumbled with the key slot. The 4.7 litre V8 caught and the truck shot out of the parking place as if it were pursued by demons snapping at its tail gate.

It seemed to Jimmy that the truck would roll over at the first corner as he gunned it through a left turn and ran the stop sign. By the next stop sign, he was calmed down enough to stop, but he still had a death grip on the steering wheel. His whole body shook and he held onto the wheel to steady himself. He kept driving, and after another ten minutes, he stopped shaking and pulled over to the side of the road. No one was following him and he had to think what to do.

First of all, Badersault sent these guys. They knew who he was, so they knew where he lived. They would go there next. That meant he couldn't go home. Secondly, they were going to kill him or beat him up so bad he'd never talk to anyone about the Liberty Bridge. But those guys were killers. He'd never been so scared. He could see it in the black guy's eyes. He was going to be dead.

But if they were going to kill him, they would kill Janice too. They might even kill the lawyer. They would kill anyone associated with the lawsuit. He knew how they worked. He reached in the glove compartment and took out his cell phone. He called Janice.

"Mrs. Brannigan," he said, still breathless, "It's me, Jimmy Reynolds. Two men just tried to beat me up, maybe worse, and I'm calling you because I know it's about the lawsuit. I know Badersault sent them."

"Oh, my God. Are you all right?"

"Yes, just scared."

"O.K. Jimmy. I want you to talk to a man who is here to protect me. Tell him what you told me."

Janice handed the phone to Sam, who was in the next room reading a magazine.

Sam identified himself and told Jimmy that he was aware of his role in the lawsuit Janice had filed. Jimmy told Sam what had happened.

Sam said, "Are you safe now?"

"I think so."

"Take down this number. I want you to call Attorney Sean Cochran tomorrow. I'll tell him you will be calling. He's Mrs. Brannigan's new lawyer."

"What happened to Roth?" Jimmy said. "He's Mrs. Brannigan's lawyer."

"You haven't heard?"

"Heard what?"

"They killed him," Sam said.

"Oh my God, I was right. They are trying to kill us all," Jimmy said.

"They're not going to kill you or anyone else," Sam said. "You just do what I tell you and you'll be safe."

"O.K." Jimmy said, dazed and almost paralyzed by fear.

"First of all, don't go home," Sam said. "When you meet with Cochran tomorrow, he will give you money to live on and a place to stay where you'll be safe. They'll be watching your house."

"I know. I won't go home. I'll do what you say," Jimmy said, scared.

"You'll be all right," Sam said. "I know how to handle this."

CHAPTER FIFTEEN

As Tim Brannigan's white Cadillac sailed through the air upside down toward the black water of the Monongahela River, Tim was trying to scream. His mouth was wide open, his eyes were bugged out, his throat was constricted and his jaw was set. But no sound would come out. On impact, it felt like Tim's shoulder and his abdomen had been ripped out. His head hit the roof and he was in a state of semi consciousness. He had no idea how long he stayed like that, but cold water was on the top of his head. It kept moving. Sloshing around. It was dark. Pitch black. He was upside down, but he didn't know that and he couldn't figure out why the floor seemed like the ceiling. Things didn't make sense. Why was it so dark? He must be dead. That was it. He was dead.

But then the water sloshed some more and he heard a slight buzzing sound. It was the fan of the car. He was alive. But where the hell was he? He was in the car, but which way was right and left. He still had no idea of being upside down. But why was his head wet? Why was water in the car?

Then he noticed the pain in his shoulder and his abdomen. His whole body weight was strained against the belt. The water was getting in his eyes. Reflexively, he reached down for the seat belt release, but he realized he was really reaching up. Up was down. Down was up. He had fallen into the river. He was upside down. This water was the river. He was going to die. The belt broke loose and he sank into the water in the top of the car. He realized that he was in an air pocket, but it was filling up with water fast.

He had to get out, but the windows were now under the water. He noticed his teeth were chattering. The water had to be fifty degrees. He would die of the cold. Hypothermia. He had to get to that window. He screwed up his courage and knelt under the water. The only way he knew which was down was that the air was on top. It was totally black and he was so disoriented that he felt his way along the door to locate the window. He banged on it with his fist. Nothing happened. He twisted his body around and kicked with his foot. Nothing happened. The air pocket now was almost gone. There was hardly enough room for him to gasp for air. The panic was now full blown. He was going to die in here. He couldn't see. He kept getting confused about which way was up. He couldn't move. He couldn't get out. He would drown.

He dove for the window. He felt the door, the seat, then the smooth glass of the window. He reached in his pocket and pulled out his pocket knife. It was a folding knife that Janice had given him. He carried it everywhere. He opened the blade and stabbed the glass as hard as he could. The glass shattered and he swam through the opening, pulling with all his strength for the surface. When his head burst through the surface, he shot up into the air like a whale, gasping and wheezing and floundering for breath . The body of the car slowly swirled downward, sinking to the depths of the river.

He was still gasping and floundering when he felt the current of the river take him. He grabbed a last mouthful of air and went under. It felt like he was in a pneumatic tube. He was sucked along, his whole body, shooting through the depths of the river to an unknown destination. My God, I'm going to drown anyway, he thought. His lungs were near the end of their air, and then past the end, and Tim knew he was dead. But then his body shot through the surface again and he blew out and sucked in air as fast as he could, crazy with fear, certain that the black muddy water was going to seize him again. He floundered and gasped.

And he was right. It seized him again, as rapidly as it had done before, and it dragged him down into its depths and this time he went deeper and deeper and the pull was terrific, even more powerful, and fast. Again, his lungs were near to bursting and he began to exhale because he couldn't hold it any longer, and once again, he was jettisoned through the surface to gasp and struggle for life.

He could feel the current on the surface this time and he could see from the lights on the shore that he was moving down the river at a fast pace. He could tread water and let the current move him along, but he was terrified that another current would drag him under. And sure enough, as he thought of it, he could feel a tug at his feet and he could feel his body being pulled down again. He kicked and struggled with what energy he had left to escape the deadly force, and he splashed and reached out with his flailing arms.

There was a sharp blow to his wrist. He had hit something in his flailing. He grabbed it. He tried to grab it. It was floating past as he was going under. It was a large tree limb. He grabbed with both hands and kicked with an adrenalin surge of energy toward the life-giving branch. He had it. He held on. He didn't go under.

The branch flew along through the night water, under bridges, past lights, alongside roads, near boulders, bumping into buoys and turning end-for-end in the current. Tim held on for almost an hour before the branch ran into a tree that had fallen from the shore and locked up in its branches. Numb and paralyzed with fear, Tim extracted himself from the water and slowly crawled along the trunk of the fallen tree until he reached the bank of the river. There he passed out. He was near death from hypothermia.

When he opened his eyes the next day, he was surrounded by strange faces and what looked like cardboard. He was piled high with dirty blankets and coats. All of the men who looked down at him were unshaven and had a hollow look. Many of them had no teeth.

"Where am I?" He said, coughing.

"You were in the river, Bucko. We pulled you out," one of them said.

"We didn't take nothin," another one said.

"You wuz a gonner, Bucko," the first one said. "A gonner."

A large man pushed some of the others aside and said, "I'm the one as pulled you out. These others, they just piled the blankets on. You wuz near dead from the cold. We couldn't build no fire cause of the police, but we put some cardboard up here to keep the cold out."

"Pretty is as pretty does," one of the men said.

"Shut the fuck up, Amos," the big man said.

"I tole you before, pretty is as pretty does," he repeated.

Some of the other men pushed him back out of the inner circle and several said, "Shut that fucker up."

The big man came forward again and said, "Look mister, we helped you as best we could, as we wuz wondering if you could help us a little."

Tim was dazed and freezing cold even under all the blankets and was about to tell them to call the police and he would pay them all whatever they wanted when it occurred to him. He would pay them, but there was no need for the police. This might be an opportunity.

CHAPTER SIXTEEN

Linda got to Tim's cardboard hospice a little after seven that evening. The bum in charge couldn't raise her on the phone until after she returned from work, and then he had trouble persuading her to come to Neville Island. Finally, she agreed to come because the bum was able to give her enough details of her personal life that she realized Tim must have told him.

When the chief bum met her at a road dead-ending into the river, he gave her Tim's watch and his wallet to induce her to follow him to the river bank, where Tim remained under the blankets. Tim had given the bum a little more than two hundred dollars to make the calls to Linda with the promise of more from a bank machine if she actually came.

Linda got everyone's attention in her bright red mini skirt and red spike heels. She had on a pink plastic raincoat and matching hat against the elements. Her shapely legs and curly blonde hair surfaced from the plastic at regular intervals and left all of the gathered bums spellbound. When she looked over top of the cardboard hospice, she gasped and dropped to her knees to reach Tim under the pile of old coats and moldy blankets. He was still coming out of shock, but he managed a smile when she reached for him. With the bums' help, she got him to her car, turned the heat up full blast, for he was still shaking from cold, and took the leader of the derelicts to a bank machine, where she got an additional three hundred dollars for him.

On the way back to her apartment, Tim, still shivering, told her as much as he knew about what had happened and she told him that she had seen the bridge collapse on the news, but she had no idea he was involved.

Tim was so cold that he was unable to feel the warmth of the car's heater. When Linda got him home, she filled the bathtub with hot water and helped him slide into it. He was still shaking with cold when he got into the tub. His teeth were chattering. Even after Tim was in the hot water for a time, he still could not feel the heat of the water. Forty-five minutes later, Tim began to have sensations of warmth and his teeth finally stopped chattering. He seemed a little less groggy than he had been and he began talking about how hungry he was.

Linda went to the kitchen and began to fix him something to eat. In a few minutes, Tim got out of the tub, exhausted but finally warm, wrapped in three blankets, and Linda fed him toast, eggs, chicken soup and coffee. She sat at the table as he ate, talking about the bums and the accident and how she couldn't believe what had happened. She couldn't believe he was here.

When he had finished the eggs and the soup, Tim began to get irritated with Linda's chattering, but then he realized he hadn't told her about his plan.

"Listen a minute, Baby. I've figured out a way for you and me to make it big."

"What are you talking about?"

"Just listen. There is a big insurance policy on me. If I stay hidden, the insurance company will assume I am dead and they'll pay three million dollars on the policy. We can go away and live like... like... millionaires."

"Yeah," she said, lighting a cigarette, a habit Tim despised, "But she'll get the money. We won't."

"Don't you worry about that. When they pay her, I'll show up and tell her we're running away, but she'll have to give me the money and keep quiet about it."

"Why would she do that?"

"Because she loves me."

"Is that how you treat women who love you?" She said.

"Come on, Linda, this is our big chance. Don't ruin it."

"I'm not ruining it, Tim, but I wonder if that's what you would do with me?"

"Honey, I love you."

"You probably love her too."

"No, I told you. I don't love her. I'm just using her to get the insurance money. Let me do this my way and we'll be able to go to Europe and live."

Four days later Brannigan's car was discovered, washed up near Neville Island. His body was missing. He saw news clips of his grief-stricken wife being hounded by reporters.

Over the next month, Tim became more intimately acquainted with the lascivious Linda. The sex was outstanding, but some of Linda's other qualities began to wear thin.

Apart from her incessant smoking, admiring herself in every mirror she walked by, and drinking too much, Linda's reading material was exclusively the tabloids from supermarkets or celebrity magazines. Not surprisingly, her conversation was reflective of her reading material. For another thing, her idea of cooking was heating up a can of soup. And finally, she dressed in cheap, tasteless clothes that showed off her body but also made her out to be either a hooker or an idiot. He hadn't noticed these things in their three month affair before he fell off the bridge. Back then, her conversation seemed full of life, they always ate out, and he spent more time with her out of her clothes than in.

Tim was wearing a bit on Linda too. She was not used to the vibes of disapproval from Tim or anyone else. She was used to being admired, sought after and made much of. Tim admired her body, but she was beginning to think he didn't like the rest of her very well. Both of them began to get testy.

"How much longer are we gonna sit around here living off my money? I don't even have enough to buy new clothes any more," she said after the second week.

"I told you, we can't do anything until she's been paid. We have to make sure she's been paid."

"How long will that be?"

"Are we there yet?"

"What?"

"Are we there yet? That's what kids say when they're riding in cars. That's what you're doing."

Increasingly, Linda began to drink more heavily of the cheap jug wine she favored. She was dissatisfied when she got home, immediately soaked in the bathtub, was surly by seven o'clock and drunk by nine.

By about eight o'clock, her conversation was typically, "You just want to fuck me. You're just a.. a... fucker. That's it. A fucker. You."

Tim put up with her outbursts and her childlike impatience largely because he couldn't think of any options. He had no money. He couldn't go to the bank machine. If he left, he wasn't sure who she would tell that he was still alive. And in any case, he had no place to go. It was turning into a bad situation. He couldn't figure out why it was so difficult for her to understand that they just needed to wait until he had been pronounced dead and the insurance company paid off. It seemed pretty simple.

In the meantime, she got up every morning and got ready for work just as if nothing had happened the night before. She was a little sluggish when she first got up, but who wasn't? By the time she got out of the shower and started her hour-long make-up routine, she was pretty much awake.

Linda had abandoned her job at the cosmetics counter of a department store and was now a receptionist at a high end law firm. She enjoyed watching all of the lawyers look at her legs. Occasionally she would catch them ogling her rear end. She loved the importance she felt working there. She was important enough that they put her out front for their rich clients to see. The rich clients liked her too. She dressed well, she thought, just like they did, but maybe a little snappier.

CHAPTER SEVENTEEN

"I seen the motherfucker, Wysorek. He's in the bitch's house right now. How about I do em both?" Morengeone said, talking into his cell phone.

Wysorek said, "Hold on." He cleared the people out of his office and closed the door.

"Now," he said, "Which motherfucker are you talking about?"

"The one that jammed the candle in my eye," Morengeone said.

"Oh, Jimmy Reynolds, the fuckin traitor," Wysorek said.

"That's him."

"Where the hell are you?" Wysorek said.

"We're at the bitch's house. You know, the lawsuit bitch. We been watchin it like we sposed to and this motherfucker comes drivin right up."

"I don t want you to lose him this time. Get that little fucker and finish him off," Wysorek said. "How far away from the house are you?"

"I'm in the fuckin woods. I'm watchin with spy glasses, just like I said I would. Where the fuck else would I be?"

"Get down there and park right outside that house so you can nab him when he comes out."

"You dumb, Wysorek. I ain't putting my black ass down in that white suburb. I may as well try sellin hot dogs at a KKK meetin. I ain't goin down there. I tole you that before. When he leaves I'll see him from up here."

"Yeah, and you'll lose him again," Wysorek said.

"If I lose him, I'll kill the bitch. That makes more sense anyway."

"Look, Fazoon, you leave the thinking to me. You just do what I say."

"Fazoon? Who you callin' Fazoon, you cracker sonofabitch?"

"Stay away from the Brannigan broad. She doesn't get touched." Wysorek said.

"Yeah, yeah, yeah." Morengeone said.

"You want paid, you do what I say," Wysorek said, and hung up.

"Huffy motherfucker," Morengeone said to the dead phone. "Fazoon," he said to himself.

Morengeone was standing alongside a fence two hundred yards from Janice's house, next to the subdivision where she lived, on a wooded hill. He and Federman had driven their car up a dirt road that went into the woods and had stopped near the edge of the woods overlooking the subdivision. There was a clear view of the front of Janice's house from here with binoculars. They had been able to observe without being observed. Federman slept in the car or listened to his iPod while Morengeone stood watch. They had been there more than eight hours before Jimmy showed up in a late model pick-up truck.

Inside the house, Jimmy was introducing himself to Janice, Sam and Ronin. He had met with Cochran several times and Janice wanted to meet him. He was what made her lawsuit possible. She wanted to thank him for coming forward and for warning her. As Janice served coffee and cookies, Sam and Jimmy talked while Jimmy petted Ronin.

Sam asked, "How's the new apartment?"

Jimmy laughed. "A lot nicer than my own," he said.

"You've lost your job," Janice said.

"Yeah, well, I wasn't doing so good there, anyway."

"When my husband died," Janice said, "I got a large insurance settlement and I'm going to give you some money so you can get along until this is over," Janice said. "I feel so bad about you're being dragged into this and those people trying to hurt you."

"I appreciate that, but I don't need money," Jimmy said.

Sam handed him a check and said, "Please take this, Jimmy. We need to have you safe and we need for you to have enough money to live while they are chasing you. I'm asking you as a favor, take it."

The check was for twenty thousand dollars. Jimmy swallowed hard and remained silent for a minute. Then he said, "This is a lot of money. What I don't need, I'll return."

"That won't be necessary," Janice said. "And if you need more, let me know. You are what makes my case work."

Sam said, "I meant to have Cochran ask you, Jimmy. Do you know a guy named Blinkman?"

"Yeah. He's an engineer. Works for PennDOT."

"Do you know if he's still there?" Sam said.

"I don't know. I used to see him on the job now and then. Seemed like a good guy."

"Would he know about what Badersault was doing on the Liberty Bridge project?"

"Oh, yeah, he was all over that construction. Just like I was. There were a lot of people who knew what Badersault was doing," Jimmy said.

"That's good," Sam said. "He might be another source of information for Janice's suit."

"He'd know a lot," Jimmy said.

When the three had finished their coffee, Jimmy rose to go.

"Thanks," Jimmy said. "I really appreciate all the support you're giving me. I'll stay in touch."

Jimmy went to his truck, which was parked on the street. When Morengeone saw him come out, he jogged to the car and roused Federman from his iPod. It was dusk.

By the time Jimmy got turned around and headed back out of the subdivision, Morengeone and Federman were on the main road approaching the entrance to the subdivision. As Morengeone approached, Jimmy pulled out, turning to the right. Jimmy noticed the headlights right away in his rear view mirror. The car behind him seemed aggressive. It was some sort of an older Cadillac or Buick.

The cloverleaf leading back to the interstate highway was not far, and Jimmy kicked down the throttle of the Toyota Tundra pickup truck. The V8 was responsive and he went into the easy curve of the cloverleaf turn onto I-79 at seventy miles an hour. He throttled up coming out of the last bend and headed north for Pittsburgh. The Cadillac was right behind him. He could see two figures in the car.

Alarmed now, Jimmy realized it must be somebody hired by Badersault to kill him. They must have been watching Janice's house. It was stupid to go there. Jimmy steered around traffic in three lanes, increasing speed. When he had woven through the cars blocking his path, Jimmy accelerated and the Toyota quickly hit a hundred and ten miles per hour. The Cadillac bobbed and swayed right behind him. Jimmy moved from lane to lane with ease shifting the big V8 down to brake for traffic ahead, running up to redline, changing lanes and then accelerating once he was in the clear. He could see clouds of smoke coming from the Cadillac. "Maybe he'll blow the engine," Jimmy thought.

No such luck. The two cars sped north at breakneck speeds, the truck solid and nimble, the Cadillac swaying dangerously and belching clouds of smoke at each difficult maneuver. Jimmy saw the Bridgeville exit coming up and switched to the right lane, swerving onto the exit at a perilously high speed. The Cadillac nearly wrecked, cutting off a car in the right lane to follow him onto the exit.

The exit was a straight ramp down to a state route, Route 51, and when Jimmy merged into 51, there was a traffic light a hundred yards ahead. It was red. Traffic was stopped five cars deep. There was a grass strip along the right side of the road leading up to the stop light, but it was bordered by a thick concrete curb that was at least eight inches high. Jimmy hit the curb where it just began to ramp up to its full eight inches.

The front end bucked over the curb and onto the grass. The rear end followed, bumping high into the air as first one tire and then the other hit the curb. Once on the grass, Jimmy passed the cars stopped at the light and bounced down off the curb, first the front, then the rear, skidding and squealing tires onto the cross-road that intersected Route 51.

Behind him he got a glimpse of the Cadillac with one wheel up on the curb, sparks flying, and then he had an image of it bumping back down into the road again. Behind him, he heard horns blowing.

Jimmy raced down the road, past houses and supermarkets set among trees. Five years ago, this had been the country. Now it was the suburbs. There were still some barns, but subdivisions of huge houses sprang up like acne among the trees. The road was curvy. He raced through a red light in front of a newly constructed supermarket.

He turned left at a two-lane road with a sign pointing to Mayview Hospital. More houses. These had been here for a long time. Little blue and yellow boxes with brown roofs. Working class places with gardens and front yards. Motorcycles and quad runners here and there in the driveways. Better slow down now, he said to himself.

Nothing behind him. Then, unbelievably, the big headlights bounced and weaved on the small road a hundred yards back. It could only be them.

To his left there was a sign for a housing development. He could see buildings. Hunting Ridge. Jimmy wheeled the big truck into the development, hoping to be far enough ahead that they would not see him turn, but, looking in the mirror, he saw the ominous lights lean at a severe angle and skid around the corner after him.

To his right, Jimmy saw a baseball field bordered by what looked like a football field, the whole thing maybe two or three hundred yards long of essentially open field, dotted here and there with obviously marshy wet spots. Jimmy slowed to approach the turnoff to the field and as he hit thirty miles per hour for the turn, he reached down and switched on four-wheel drive.

The big car slid into the turn behind him and both vehicles accelerated toward the baseball diamond, which was, as Jimmy now saw, essentially mud. He hit the infield at forty miles an hour and felt the truck start to slide. It was as if he had hit ice. Feathering the throttle, he pulled out more or less straight and headed for the football field. The football field was a little more solid, but when he hit the marshy areas, he felt the truck slide sideways and backed off the throttle in order to steer out of the skid.

Jimmy glanced at the mirror and instantly broke out into a guffaw as he saw that the big car was stopped in the middle of the baseball infield and two figures were standing outside of the car. Jimmy slowed and found the quickest way off the field, then back onto the subdivision road, then out to the country road and freedom. He realized that he was covered with sweat. "Jesus Christ," he murmured.

Wiping his face on his sleeve and his hands on his pants, he willed his heart to slow down a little and he took some deep breaths. He wiped his brow again with his shirt sleeve and pulled out the cell phone. Sam answered.

"Sam, this is Jimmy."

"What's up, Jimmy?"

"I just got chased by two guys in a Cadillac. We were going down I-79 at over a hundred miles an hour and the only way I could get away from them was to drive across a field where they got stuck. I'm somewhere near Bridgeville."

"O.K. Do you need help?"

"No. I got away for now. They're back there stuck.

But I thought you'd want to know."

"They must have been watching the house," Sam said. "Thanks for the warning. Since they didn't get you, they may have some ideas about coming back here. You sure you're O.K.?"

"Yeah. You want me to come back there"

"No. Go to your motel and stay out of sight. I'll talk to you tomorrow."

CHAPTER EIGHTEEN

Sam called Nick and told him what had happened. Nick loaded Cochran in the car and headed for Janice's house. By the time he arrived, forty-five minutes later, it was dark. Nick and Cochran parked on a side road and bushwhacked into Janice's back yard. If someone was watching the house, there was no point in advertising that they had arrived. Nick called Sam to tell him they were in the back yard and Sam let them in the darkened kitchen door.

Sam and Nick took up defensive positions covering the front and back entrances and put Janice and Cochran in a bedroom on the second floor. Lights were out everywhere except in the living room, where three lamps were turned on and the heavy drapes were pulled. The construction of the house was concrete block faced with brick, which meant that Janice and Cochran should be safe from even heavy caliber fire while lying on mattresses on the floor near the inner walls. Cochran was familiar with pump shotguns, so Nick gave him an Ithaca Model 37, military issue, with a magazine tube extending the full length of the eighteen inch barrel. It was stoked with double ought buckshot. A bandolier of extra loads lay on the floor next to the gun.

Ronin roamed the inner perimeter of the house, listening for sounds outside. His hearing was so acute that he could detect a man moving in the yard. Sam was in a corner of the living room where he could respond to entry either from the front door or through the picture window in the front of the house.

Separating him from Nick was the wooden cabinetry that divided the kitchen from the living room. The kitchen was dark and Nick was in a corner of the kitchen covering entry from the kitchen door or window. He was hunkered down behind an antique maple wash stand that was made with solid two inch planks. He could cover Sam's back from there simply by pivoting around and standing up.

All four defenders had gas masks in the unlikely event of a gas canister lobbed through a window, and Sam and Nick wore protective goggles treated to deaden the blinding effects of flash-bang grenades. They also had ear-defender headsets that allowed them to communicate in whispers and protected them from loud noises from gunfire or explosion. They were ready.

About two a.m. a car pulled up outside and parked in front of Janice's house. It sat there for a few minutes. Nick watched through a darkened window in the front of the house. Two figures finally got out.

"They're here," Nick said into the headset. "Nothing too subtle."

He watched as the two men walked up the driveway toward the front door.

"I think they're coming to the front door, for Christ's sake."

"Get ready to cover the back in case it s a ruse," Sam said.

Nick took up a position in the dark, shotgun shouldered, watching the back door. Sam stayed where he was in the living room. He had an M4 rifle loaded with fifty-five grain ball. The selector was set on full auto.

Ronin was in the living room. He had alerted to sounds outside and he looked to Sam for direction. Sam gave a hand signal for Ronin to move toward the sound to see whether they were where he thought they were. Ronin went to the font door. Sam moved out of the living room, almost back to back with Nick, where he was in line with the front door, and signaled for Ronin to come back. He was concerned they would shoot through the door or blow it with explosives and he wanted Ronin at a safe distance.

Nothing happened for two minutes, and then there was a loud pounding on the door. The doorbell began to ring.

"Watch the back," Sam whispered. "I'll see what's out there."

Sam moved toward the front door and stepped to the side. He had a fiber optic tube hooked up to the peek hole which allowed him to see who was outside from the side of the door.

Ronin stayed back with Nick, watching intently as Sam approached the side of the door. Through the fiber optic tube Sam saw two men, one a hulking black man with yellow canine teeth and the other a bulldozer on legs.

"Looks like Fang and the wrecking ball have arrived," Sam whispered into the headset. "They're both here. Must be the same guys who came after Jimmy in that bar."

More pounding came on the door. Then a deep voice.

"We knows you be in there, bitch. Let nice Bartholomew in to talk to you. I'm freezing like a motherfucker out here."

This was followed by more pounding.

"Come on bitch. We knows you scared and all, but Bartholomew be here to fix all that shit up. Open the doe."

Sam whispered, "I'm gonna open the door, Nick. Keep your eye on the back until you hear things happening in front. If they have somebody in the back stay with that. I'll have Ronin give the greeting."

"Acknowledged," Nick said, chuckling.

Staying to the side of the door, Sam continued to monitor the two men. No weapons were showing. Pretty cocky. Maybe they don't know we're here. They think she's here by herself. Staying to the side of the door and continuing to watch, Sam loudly snicked one of the deadbolts open. The two men stopped pounding. Still no weapons. They just stood there. Sam gave a hand signal to Ronin, who got to his feet and stood ten feet back from the door. Sam snicked the last deadbolt and jerked the door open toward him so that he was behind it.

As soon as Morengeone was visible through the open door, Ronin was launched. The speed with which he shot through the air was astounding. He was a hundred and fifty pound bullet.

As Ronin was in mid-air, Sam heard, "Sheeeeit" from Morengeone just before Ronin's paws hit him full in the chest. The impact of the muscular dog was so powerful that Morengeone fell back into Federman, his arms flailing to protect his face. As soon as Ronin hit, he seized on one of the flailing wrists and broke the bone just as Morengeone 's legs collapsed under the unexpected weight of the dog on his chest. The two men hit the ground with the dog on top of them. Instantly, Ronin released the mangled broken wrist and pivoted behind Morengeone, standing on Federman's face and clamping down on Morengeone's shoulder.

Morengeone bellowed with pain. Ronin's teeth now were sunk into the top of his collar bone, and he was shaking his powerful head, lifting Morengeone's entire torso off the ground as he did. Akitas have locking jaws. The jaws were locked.

"Federman, get the motherfucker. Get the motherfucker. Get the motherfucker off me. For Christ's sake. Owwwwwww. Goddam it. Morengeone was pounding on the top of the dog's head with his one good arm with no apparent effect.

Sam had rounded the door and was covering both men with the M4 rifle.

Federman pushed Ronin to the side and got to his feet. He glanced at Sam and the rifle, then he reached down and grabbed Ronin by the neck. Sam drew a bead on Federman's head at a distance of five feet, but Ronin was in the way. At first when Federman grabbed him, Ronin maintained his grip on Morengeone 's shoulder, and then suddenly, Federman actually jerked him loose.

Sam saw blood on Ronin's snout as Federman lifted him into the air and held him at arm's length, blocking Sam's shot. The big dog was twisting, growling and snapping as only a hundred and fifty pound Akita can do. Sam waited, anticipating that Federman would throw Ronin to the side and open himself to a clear shot.

But that didn't happen. Instead, Federman continued to hold the dog in front of his body, swinging him back and forth. Ronin squirmed, twisted, did bending contortions with his body, all the while growling and foaming at the mouth. He swung his great body in arcs and scratched deep gouges in Federman's belly with his claws. The entire front of Federman's shirt went red with his own blood. Ronin's teeth snapped and clicked as he made lunges for Federman's throat.

Even though Federman had Ronin in a powerful grip, he almost lost his hold several times, and when he did, Ronin got close enough to bite. Once, he grabbed Federman's face and ripped a gaping hole in his right cheek; another time he bit Federman's chin and lips and the space below his nose. All of the facial wounds were bleeding profusely, but Federman held on. Blood flowed in a wide stream down Federman's face, onto his neck and into his shirt. Ronin's growling was fierce, but now it was also distressed, and he seemed to have trouble breathing. His twisting was becoming less violent. It was time for Sam to move.

Morengeone seemed unable to move. But he was a possible problem, and Sam kicked him in the head as he stepped towards Federman. The kick knocked him unconscious. Stepping over Morengeone 's body, Sam approached the struggling Ronin and Federman. Federman saw him coming and moved so that the body of the dog was between him and Sam. Ronin thrashed and growled and Sam could see glimpses of the bleeding face behind the body of the dog.

Without consciously deciding what he would do, Sam fired a five round burst at Federman's feet. The muzzle blast was deafening and hot brass flew out the side of the M4. Before Sam realized what was happening, Federman threw the dog at Sam. Ronin's squirming body hit Sam, knocking him backwards and momentarily the muzzle of Sam's rifle was tangled up in Ronin's churning legs. Sam struggled to regain his balance and Ronin skittered off to the side. Now Sam perceived things moving in slow motion. Ronin regained his feet and circled instantly to get behind Federman. In Sam's mind, he moved in great slow gallops, one frame at a time, circling back to Federman and driving his two inch fangs into the big man's thigh. Sam saw Federman's slow motion flinch when the dog clamped down. He saw Federman's bloody shirt. He saw the mangled face. He saw the dead eyes, and he saw, ever so slowly, the massive fist coming at him. The knuckles were logs. He was about to be hit by something rivaling the power of a falling tree. He raised the butt of the rifle to block the blow as best he could, but the rifle weighed two hundred pounds and came up ever so slowly. Inexorably, the fist kept coming, always in slow motion, and knocked the rifle into Sam's face. Sam fell backwards, only it was falling in slow motion. Dear God, he thought, let me hang on to the gun. As Sam fell, there were two loud explosions.

Nick was standing over the prostrate Sam with the Benelli M1 shotgun pointing downward at what had been Federman's face. Nick had seen Federman pick Ronin up and toss him away like a stuffed animal. Federman didn't react to Ronin's bites, even bites to his face, and he hit Sam with enough force to take him down. It was clear to Nick that the situation was serious and nothing short of double ought buckshot to the head was going to stop Federman, and he wasn't even sure about that.

When Nick shot Federman, the big man stood for a few seconds on his feet. He was literally dead on his feet and most of his head had been blown away, shot at a distance of three feet by a twelve gauge shotgun loaded with 00 buck. Nonetheless, what was left of him continued standing while Ronin renewed his attack on Federman's leg, jaws locked, growling, and shaking his massive head. Then Federman fell. Ronin scampered out from under the falling body and moved between Sam and Morengeone, growling the low menacing growl. Morengeone couldn't move. He sat on the ground holding his blood-soaked shoulder with his good hand while the hand with the broken wrist dangled by his side.

Nick helped Sam to his feet, and when Sam's head cleared, the two of them helped Morengeone limp into the house.

Inside, Sam told him to lie on the floor spread-eagled. Bartholomew's shoulder didn't work right, but he did the best he could. His driver's license gave an obviously bogus address, 234 Main Street, and the improbable name Bartholomew Morengeone. Apart from money, a cell phone and a large folding knife, that's all there was.

"What were you gonna do, scare us with that big knife?" Nick said.

"Nobody said nothing about no wild-ass crackers and a bear bein' here," Morengeone said. "The only white boy I saw come in here already left, and bears ain't allowed in the city. I'da known, I'da brought a piece and killed yo' white asses and the bear too."

Nick butt-stroked him with the shotgun as he sat on the floor, knocking him back down with a bloody mouth. Ronin growled.

"Talk nice, insect, and maybe you'll live through the night," Nick said.

"Who sent you?" Sam said.

"You gonna kill me?"

"Not unless you give me a reason," Sam said.

"How I do that?"

"Don't tell me what I ask you."

"Oh." Pause. "You know who sent me. The bridge doctors."

"Give me a name."

"Wysorek."

"He in your cell phone?"

"Yee."

"What?"

"Yee."

"I think that's 'yes,'" Nick said.

Sam looked through the directory and came to Wysorek's name. He dialed. Wysorek must have had caller ID because he answered, "It's about time you called. I pay your black ass to do what I say, not do it when you feel like it. You hear?"

"My name is John Donne," Sam said.

There was silence on the other end of the phone.

"You sent two goons to my client's house to kill her," he continued. "Instead, we killed one of them and the other one is sitting here in bad shape. I'm sending the one with yellow teeth back to you with the body of the Neanderthal. I'll tell you this once, so listen. If you send this guy after my client again, or if you send anyone else, I will put a bullet in your head."

Sam hung up, handed the phone to Morengeone, and told him to put the phone and the other stuff back in his pockets.

"I like that," Morengeone said. "I put a bullet in yo head. Should'a tole that honky motherfucker that myself."

Morengeone, using his one good arm, and Nick dragged the body of Federman back to Morengeone 's car while Sam covered them with the shogun.

Morengeone started the engine and Sam leaned in the passenger side. "Those teeth of yours. Get some white strips," he said.

CHAPTER NINETEEN

Janice, Cochran, Sam and Nick sat in a bunkerized kitchen eating eggs and bacon and discussing the last night's adventures. Heavy furniture was piled up in front of any glass openings and the blinds were drawn so that targets could not be acquired from outside. Ronin patrolled the inner perimeter of the house, listening for outside sounds. A TV monitor which Sam and Nick had hooked up belatedly last night showed the four sides of the house, the street and the woods behind the house. Nick and Sam both automatically glanced at the screens as they ate and talked.

"Are you sure that man was dead?" Janice said.

"He was dead," Sam said.

"I'm so sorry I got you into this," Janice said.

"This is what we do for a living, Janice," Sam said. "If Nick hadn't shot him, there's a good chance he would have killed us both."

"But shouldn't the police be involved?" She whimpered.

"You can call the police if you want, but then Nick and I are out of here. We don't work with the police. They will tie our hands and make it impossible for us to protect you," Sam said.

Cochran said, "Sam's right, Janice. The cops are bureaucrats. There's not an ounce of sense among them. They'll be in here wanting to see licenses and confiscating guns and arresting Sam and Nick, maybe charging them, maybe not, and costing you ten or twenty thousand dollars in legal fees."

The phone rang. Probably more threats. Nick activated a tape recorder and Sam picked up a second handset when Janice answered.

"Hello?" She said, tentatively.

"Hello, Baby, it's me. It's Tim."

Janice's eyes instantly brimmed full of tears and her eyes sprung to life, wide open.

"Tim, Timmy, is it you?"

"Yes, Baby, I'm all right."

"No, but they told me... the police told me you were dead," she said.

"I've been hiding out. I didn't want anyone to know I was alive," he said.

"But Tim, why didn't you tell me? Why did you let me go through this terrible thing?"

"I had to, honey. I had to for the insurance money. I was going to..."

Sam had ended the connection. Janice looked at Sam with stricken eyes. "But why...?"

"Listen to me," Sam said firmly, "And do exactly what I tell you. He will call back. When he does, tell him you can't talk now, but you want him to come here tomorrow night. Tell him the newspaper reporters have been hanging around, but it will be safe by then."

"But why? It's Tim. I need to talk to him. Oh my God, it's Tim. He's alive!"

"Janice," Sam said, "I know this is hard for you, but listen to me. It's possible to change voices on the telephone. Maybe it's Tim, maybe it isn't. I want you to ask him a question that only you and he know the answer to."

"O.K. But it's him. I just know it."

"Even if it is," Sam said. "We still have to be careful. You are paying us to protect you and so I expect you to listen to me. We have to be careful because we don't know why he hadn't told you he was alive before this."

"Yes, but I'm sure there is a good reason," Janice said.

"I'm sure there is," Sam said. "But here's what you have to do. Ask him the question that only you know the answer to and then tell him that he can come over tomorrow night, but not before."

The phone rang. It was Tim. Janice struggled. She needed Tim to come over right then, but she did as Sam asked and set up a meeting for the next night.

"I need to see you now, Honey," he said.

"I know, Tim, I need to see you too. But it's not safe here now. There's too much going on. The newspaper reporters are still hanging around. Sometimes they just stop over. I'll tell you about it tomorrow. Just do it tomorrow. All right? I don't want to wait either, but do it tomorrow."

"Tomorrow. . . Tomorrow. I can't believe this, Honey, I need to see you now," he sulked.

Then she asked him, "Tim, do you remember where we went for our last anniversary? The place with the little band?"

The phone was silent for a minute. Tim had put the entire world of his marriage to Janice out of his mind. And then he remembered. "Oh, yeah, the Mexican place. Tina's Grill," he said.

"Yes," she said. "It really is you."

"Of course it is, Baby. What do you mean? Can't you tell it's me?

Sam made a signal and she said, "Tim, I can't talk now. Just come tomorrow. I can't wait."

When she hung up, Janice slumped into a chair and put her face in her hands and sobbed.

The three men looked at each other.

"This changes things," Sam said.

When Janice regained some of her composure, Sam said, "Are you sure it's him?"

"Oh, yes. It's Tim," she said. "I'm sure."

"Then I'm sure you're right, Janice, but we have to be careful here because we don't know exactly why he has pretended to be dead and what the consequences will be."

Corcoran said, "For one thing, the police will want to know why he pretended to be dead. For another, the insurance companies will want their money back. And for another, there will be complications at your husband's business because you already sold his interest for a million dollars and they may have divided that interest among other partners. And finally, you are in the midst of a life and death struggle with somebody who wants to kill you because you are suing him and revealing his corrupt business practices, because he has — supposedly — killed your husband. Except your husband isn't dead."

"I don't care about any of that," Janice said. "I just want to be with my husband."

"I understand," Sam said, "But if we aren't careful, he will go to jail and you will be penniless or dead."

"And then you wouldn't be with him," Nick said, "And you wouldn't have any way to help him."

She said, "All right, I'll listen to what you have to say."

"I have a plan," Sam said. "I think it may be time to have a conversation with the Count von Badersault."

CHAPTER TWENTY

"Mr. Count," Bobby Lee ventured, seeing that his boss, Wolfgang Badersault, was reading the paper.

Glaring, cold eyes emerged over the top of the paper. Badersault's enormous head appeared in full as the paper was lowered enough to show the entire face. The bulbous lips and ulta-wide mouth made him seem almost like a cartoon character.

"How many times I told ya, Bobby Lee, it's not 'Mr. Count,' it's 'Count.'"

"Yes, Count," Bobby Lee apologized, hat in hand. Bobby Lee was the foreman of the Badersault estate, formally known as Badersault Hall.

"Well, what is it?"

"I just came to tell you, just so's you'd know, Mr. Count, it's the crim'nals..."

"Goddam it to hell, Bobby Lee, it's 'Count,' 'Count,' got it?"

"Yessir, Mr. Badersault, I mean, Count."

"Now what about criminals?"

"Well, sir, it's the crim'nals. You said the sheriff was going to send over some deputies to polish cars, but instead he sent a bunch a crim'nals. I just thought you'd wanta know. Cause it's crim'nals on them cars."

"How many criminals we talking about?"

"Well sir, I'd say they's got to be thirty of 'em. And some of them, well sir, they the meanest looking motherfuckers I ever did see."

"Is LeRoy down there with them?"

"Yes sir, he is."

"You send him on up here."

Ten minutes later a Washington County Deputy Sheriff came onto the patio where Badersault still read the paper, his feet up on a chaise lounge, his body wrapped in his bathrobe. The deputy held his hat in his hand.

"Mr. Badersault, Sir," the deputy said.

The paper lowered again and the gray eyes glared out.

"Leroy, what the hell's the sheriff mean sendin criminals over here to work on my cars. You know what that collection of cars is worth?"

"No sir, I don't, but it's a lot."

"Damn straight it's a lot. And it's too damned much to have criminals workin on it," and here the paper came all the way down. "These criminals think an exotic car is a Cadillac and their idea of takin care of it is not having any bullet holes in the trunk."

"Well, sir, I'm sure you're right about that, and what's worse is these guys would fuckin slit your throat soon's take a piss, Mr. Badersault."

The paper came back up. The voice behind the paper said, "Then you go back on down there, Leroy, and you get them criminals outa my place. When I ask the sheriff for some deputies to do some work around the place, I don't expect him to be sendin me a bunch a criminals. You tell him that, now, you hear?"

The paper came down again. The gray eyes glared out.

"Yessir, yer honor, "I'll tell him."

Badersault put the paper down and sipped his coffee. He had tasted everything in life and it was bitter. He was unhappy. He was dissatisfied. He was, of course, of noble ancestry. Maybe only a nobleman could understand what he was going through. Maybe he would go to Europe where they appreciated such things. Secretly, however, he knew they would laugh at him there. He was an American, no matter who his ancestors were, and they hated him. They would bow and scrape and take his money and laugh at him. They would call him 'Fritz' as some of them did around here. Or they would call him 'Count' and make a knowing face to their friends.

So travel wouldn't help and the domestic scene wasn't promising. Badersault's son was a drunk and a gambler, and the only time he spoke to his father was when he needed to be bailed out of some gambling debt. Badersault was at the point of wondering why he had ever baled him out. Just let them kill him. If he were dead, at least Badersault would be spared these confrontations.

His daughter married the son of a cop she met in college at the University of Pittsburgh. Last year, they moved to Alaska. But even when they were here, his relationship with the girl was strained. She seemed to think he was a bore and a bigot.

His wife, of course, was long gone. They had divorced fifteen years ago and the children had largely grown up with her. She raped him for several million in alimony and child support and he paid it just to avoid having to fight with her. She was remarried and seemed to be doing a lot better than he was.

Badersault's sex life was mostly expensive hookers. For years he had them carted out to the mansion, and he could see their eyes light up when they walked into the enormous house. Girls who had never before thought of marriage, suddenly were moonstruck. There was money in them halls. This reaction, of course, had not escaped Badersault's notice. They were there for the money — as much of it as they could get — and not for him. Somehow, that took the zing out of the sex.

The only exception he could think of was Federman. In an odd way, Wally Federman was the only human being he could even remotely say was close to him. He may seem like a human wrecking ball to some people, but he was almost like a friend to Badersault.

Morengeone used to say that in a good month, Federman would say half a dozen words, and he seemed to think that was funny. But to Badersault, that just made Federman special. He wasn't out to get anything. He was just what he was and he didn't need to talk about it. Sometimes he would hang around with Badersault, the two of them sitting in the den with the Count drinking Scotch and Federman drinking Kool-Aid, while the Count read the paper and Federman stared at the fire or the books on the shelves.

These were the things that went through the Count's mind as he lay on the chaise lounge, alone on the patio. The phone next to his chair rang and he automatically picked it up.

"Yeah," he said.

"Thought you'd want to know Mr. Badersault..."

"Well, goddam it, spit it out man..."

"Federman's dead."

CHAPTER TWENTY-ONE

On Monday morning, the day after the phone call, Badersault drove into the Liberty Bridge Construction site. The stretch limousine pulled up to the superintendent's trailer and Badersault opened his own door, stepping out into the mud. Wearing a dark suit and a gray herringbone light overcoat with a black velvet collar, Badersault gave an imperial wave to some of the men in the yard and then went into the trailer.

Inside, the obese Wysorek sat behind a messy desk. File cabinets and steel book cases overflowing with papers stood here and there in the room. A secretary sat in another room of the trailer and pecked on an old IBM Selectric typewriter. The sound of the keys striking the paper was audible when Badersault came in.

"Hello, Orey," he said, throwing some papers on the floor that had been sitting in his specially reserved overstuffed chair. There was an edge to his voice. He was subconsciously holding Wysorek responsible for Federman's death. Why the hell did he send them out to Janice's house?

"Morning, Mr. Badersault," Oregon Wysorek said, his jowls wobbling as he spoke.

The mess and Wysorek's obesity added to Badersault's anger. "Why doesn't the man take care of himself?" He thought.

Badersault sat in his chair and said, "Ask the girl to wait outside."

"Marie," Wysorek said. "Take a break. We need some privacy here. I'll call you when you can come back."

When the secretary was gone, Badersault said, "What the fuck happened?"

"I sent the nigger and Federman out to kill the traitor, you know, Jimmy Reynolds, and they chased him, but they lost him, and without me knowing it, they went back to the broad's house and decided they were going to kill her."

"We said we wasn't going to kill the broad."

"I know, Mr. Badersault, but it's that nigger. I told him, but he just does what he wants."

"Yeah? And how's Wally end up dead?"

"The broad, she wasn't alone. There were two guys and some big-ass dog there."

"Yeah, so what? Federman can lift a car full of people and squeeze them to death between the doors."

"Well, the nigger says that when the door opened, this big ass dog jumps out and grabs him by the throat and he falls into Federman and they both fall down."

"Federman falls down?"

"That's what he said. And then Federman gets the dog off of him, but one of the guys in the house comes out with a machine gun and shoots."

"So they killed him with a machine gun?"

"No. The second guy who comes out has a shotgun, and they killed him with that."

"Jesus. What's the nigger doing while their killing Federman?"

"The dog busted his wrist and tore up his shoulder and he's lying on the ground. Oh, and the guy with the machine gun kicked him in the head and he's got a concussion."

"I can't believe this."

"Yeah, and then after they killed Federman, one of these guys gets the nigger's phone and he calls me up."

"What the hell did he say?"

"He said if I ever sent anybody to get the woman again, he would kill me."

Badersault guffawed. "Some balls. I like that."

Badersault put on an appearance of not caring what happened to the two hired killers he employed, but he was grieving. Federman was dead. He could see them both sitting in the den with the fire going. Federman with his Kool-Aid, not talking, just keeping company with Badersault. Then at some point, Federman would nod his head and just leave. His death was going to leave a hole in Badersault's life.

But grief was a foreign emotion to Badersault, and he struggled to know what to do. Finally, he turned to the only thing he knew — business. Badersault and Wysorek discussed the seriousness of the threat of the Brannigan woman's lawsuit and the probabilities of getting a new contract to fix the fallen bridge. Every fifteen minutes, the scrawny Count would eat two bites of a sandwich and drink some coffee. They discussed who they would have to pay off to get another state contract, and how they could minimize the bad publicity coming from Janice's suit about the cheap steel, the bad welds and the defective concrete of their previous work. And finally, they discussed how to deal with Janice Brannigan's protectors.

As Wysorek and Badersault were talking, the phone rang and Wysorek answered. It was Sam. He was calling for Badersault.

"This is Count Wolfgang Badersault."

"This is Sam Budda, Mr. Badersault..."

"Count Badersault."

"You call yourself whatever you want, Badersault. I'm calling you to arrange a meeting to resolve our differences."

"You kill my man, you insult me with your impertinence, and then you talk about resolving our differences."

"I think you know that your man was there to kill my client. If that had not been his purpose, he would not have ended up dead. As it was, I had no choice."

"Get on with it, Budda. What do you want?"

"I want to meet with you. Arsenal Park. Eight o'clock in the morning. The bench near the dry concrete pond."

"I'll be there."

The phone went dead.

* * *

The next morning was cold for Pittsburgh in mid-summer. Fifty-nine degrees and overcast. Sam sat on the bench by the pond. Nick was seventy-five yards away with a Steyr Aug in a long gym bag. Both wore protective vests. Sam was dressed in his safari coat with a Les Baer .45 on his right hip and a titanium Smith and Wesson .357 five-shot revolver in a Thad Rybka cross- draw holster. Cross-draw holsters are not generally used by gunfighters, but they are fast from a seated position.

At eight a.m. exactly Badersault's limousine drove up to the park entrance and pulled into the park on the sidewalk. A large man got out, looked Sam's way, scanned the area, and opened the door for Badersault.

Badersault's head seemed to wobble on top of the thin body as if someone had screwed the wrong head onto the body. His puffed up facial features were prominent and he walked toward Sam with a limping gait that sometimes had a little shuffle in it. The big man followed.

Sam rose as Badersault approached.

"You the killer?" A harsh voice rasped.

"Tell the big man to go back to the car," Sam said.

"He stays."

"Then you talk to yourself," Sam said.

Badersault stared at Sam with a ferocity that seemed incongruous given his emaciated body.

"Why?"

"I don't want to be shot in the back," Sam said.

"I don't want to be killed by a killer," Badersault said.

"If I intended to kill you, you'd be dead," Sam said.

Badersault stared again. Some of his resolve seemed to be waning. Suddenly, he flicked a dismissive hand at the big man, who then turned and went to the car. He stood next to the door, watching.

"Inside the car," Sam said.

Badersault turned and made a twirling motion, and the big man got in the car.

"Satisfied?"

"Yes," Sam said.

"You've killed one of my men. I should kill you for that," Badersault said.

"If you came out here to make threats, you are wasting your time and mine," Sam said.

"If that woman you are protecting doesn't back off that lawsuit, I'm going to kill you both," Badersault said, matter of factly.

"We don't need to discuss your killing us both because I think we can probably give you what you want," Sam said.

Badersault looked at Sam, surprised. His lips moved back and forth, as if they were scrubbing themselves, searching for dirt that had settled unnoticed.

"What is it you think I want?"

"You want this lawsuit to be over."

"That would be nice."

"Of course," Sam continued, "It will cost you."

"All business costs," Badersault said.

"Three million dollars," Sam said.

Badersault snorted. "I guess you and your client will be dead."

"That's always a possibility," Sam said, "But you need to hear the rest of the proposal."

"I'm listening."

Sam handed Badersault a sheaf of ten pages, stapled in five-page groups.

"Exhibit A," Sam said, "Are the books on the Liberty Bridge job that you show the IRS and the Department of Transportation. Exhibit B are the books that show your actual expenses and profits."

Badersault examined the documents.

"Where did you get this?" He hissed.

"I have a mole in your organization, obviously," Sam said. "It isn't important who. All I need to know from you is whether you want me to release these books to the feds and get the mole into a witness protection program or whether you want to come to an understanding."

Badersault folded the papers and put them in his inside pocket.

"So in answer to the question about what you want, I think it is safe to say that you would also like these two sets of books to remain your little secret from the IRS."

Badersault remained quiet for a moment, and then said, "A million is all you get."

"Look, Fritz," Sam smiled, "This isn't negotiable. Even if you could kill me right now, these papers would be automatically sent to the authorities. And you'd still have to worry about that lawsuit. Even if you could kill the woman, her estate would continue the suit and a lawyer would be appointed by the court to do it. The allegations are already of public record, the case has already been filed. Right now, nobody but you and me and the court knows what's in that complaint because the case hasn't come to trial and nobody's had any reason to look. You kill her and the complaint gets spread all over."

"And then I'm out of business."

"And then you're in jail," Sam corrected. "And out of business."

"I like your ruthlessness, Mr. ahhhhh"

"Budda."

"Oh yes. Mr. Budda."

There was a pause. Badersault scanned Sam's face.

"You seem to have the upper hand," Badersault said.

"So it would seem," Sam said.

"You're a little cocky aren't you?"

"Not at all. It's just that I would be a fool to walk into this meeting without a way to walk out."

"I see," Badersault said.

"Most people don't do their homework. I put myself in your situation and try to decide what I would do," Sam said.

"And what would you do?"

"I'd pay. It's cheaper than the alternatives."

'What makes you think I would agree with that?"

"You're a businessman who has made millions of dollars. You don't get to that place in life if you're unable to calculate costs and benefits," Sam said.

"Three million will buy a lot of hired killers," Badersault said.

"Even if you killed me, you would still have the bad publicity, the lawsuit, and the feds going after your books," Sam said. "And if the killers got caught or killed, they would lead the police back to you."

There was another pause, a silence. Badersault studied the empty concrete pond, the maple and elm trees swaying in the breeze, and finally he said, "Three million. My lawyer will draw up the papers."

"No," Sam said. "Our lawyer has already drawn up a release. Here it is. It's simple. It says that in exchange for three million dollars Janice Brannigan releases you and Badersault Construction and anyone employed by you from any and all claims she may have now or in the future for damages she claims in her wrongful death lawsuit due to the death of her husband."

"Give it to me and my lawyer will read it over."

"Call me when you're ready. I'll meet with you or your lawyer at Mellon Bank and we will do a wire transfer of the money."

Badersault made a hummmmmpf sound and got up, staring down at Sam with his oversized head and his cold grey eyes. The door of the limousine opened and the big man got out. Suddenly, Badersault looked like an old man. "I still may kill you," he said, over his shoulder.

Sam smiled.

CHAPTER TWENTY-TWO

Sam and Nick had been watching the monitors showing the area around the house for almost three hours. Ronin made a wide sweep around the house every forty-five minutes, going into the woods behind the house and into the construction shells around the house. The cameras had infrared sensors and thermal imaging capability. If the cameras and Ronin didn't see it, it wasn't there.

This was a belt and suspenders approach, but Sam was nervous. Tim was scheduled to show up in a few hours and it was uncertain what this meant or who Tim might be working with. It was also right after Badersault had agreed to pay three million dollars. There may or may not have been a connection.

Tim arrived at seven o'clock. He drove a Volkswagen Beetle with flowers up on the dashboard and parked in the driveway.

When he rang the bell, Nick opened the door, reached out with his left hand, grabbed Tim's left upper arm and performed an arm bar over rib cage leading to a hartzel and then a takedown. Tim went "Ooof." The wind was knocked out of him when he hit the floor.

When Tim's eyes opened, he was looking in the barrel of a twelve gauge shotgun three inches from his nose. Sam held the gun on him while Nick patted him down for weapons.

"All clear," Nick said.

Nick got to his feet and extended a hand down to Tim, whose eyes were very large.

"Who the fuck are you?" He said to both Sam and Nick.

"We've been hired to protect your wife," Sam said, lowering the shotgun.

"Well, I'm her husband, idiot," Tim said.

Sam grabbed him around the throat with his free hand, the shotgun in the other, and jammed him against the wall, lifting him up on his toes.

"I'll tell you this once. If you get disrespectful, this visit will be difficult for you," Sam said.

Behind him, Janice was screaming. "Let him go, Sam. Let him go." She ran to her husband and threw her arms around his neck, pushing Sam away. The two embraced and she kissed him all over his face. Tim glared at Sam over her shoulder. Sam went into the living room to wait, and finally, Janice led Tim into the living room with Nick following.

"Here are the rules for this visit..." Sam said.

"You don't give me rules," Tim shot out. "In fact you just get the fuck out of my house."

"If I get out of your house," Sam said, "Before I go, I have to call the police."

"No. If you're going, I won't press any charges. I won't have you arrested," Tim said.

"The police are not for me," Sam said. "They're for you. I can't leave your wife here alone with you without them knowing you're alive and back in your house. That way, if something happens to her, they'll know where to look."

"That's crazy. Why would I hurt my wife?" Tim said.

"Why would you pretend you're dead?" Sam said.

"That's none of your business," Tim said.

"As long as we work for your wife, it's our business. She can fire us any time, but you can't. And if we get fired, the police get called," Sam said. "And I suspect that's a problem for you."

"Why do you say that?" Tim said.

"Because I think this is all about the three million in insurance money that your wife collected," Sam said.

"Jesus Christ," Tim glared at his wife, "Is there any thing you didn't tell them?"

"Kind of struck a nerve, huh?" Sam said.

"Janice, I need to talk to you alone," Tim said. "Tell your bodyguards to take a break, will you?"

"That's what I was trying to tell you when you interrupted me," Sam said. "There are rules. And one of them is that for this visit, we stay here while you talk to your wife."

"You can't keep me from my wife," Tim shouted.

"You can always call the police if you think we're doing something wrong," Sam said.

"Look," Nick said. "We aren't your enemy unless you make us your enemy. We have a job to do. We're protecting your wife. There's already been one attempt on her life."

"What?" Tim said, dumbfounded. "Why?"

"Because she thought you were dead," Sam said, "And she sued the contractor that worked on the bridge that killed you, and he doesn't like being sued."

"You don't kill somebody because they sue you," Tim said.

"You do if you stole millions of dollars from the state by shorting the materials on the repair," Sam said, "And you don't want this found out and broadcast all over in a lawsuit."

Tim looked at his wife and held her hand. "I had no idea," he said.

"I know," she said.

"And that brings us to why you're here," Sam said. "My guess is that you want Janice to run away with you and keep your being alive a secret."

"Yeah," Tim glared, "And you're going to screw that up, aren't you?"

Sam said, "I don't care what you do and I don't care anything about the insurance company or you committing a crime, but I do still work for your wife, and as long as that is the case, I intend to make sure that whatever you are proposing is safe for her to do."

"Is that right, Janice?" Tim said. "Are you making this guy — these guys — part of our private lives?"

"Oh, Timmy. I'm sorry. But people have been trying to kill me and if these two men had not been here, I would be dead right now. So, yes. I am. And as Sam said, he's on our side. He doesn't care about the police or the insurance company. He's not going to interfere in our lives."

"Bullshit," Tim spat out, "I'll bet you're paying him a shitload of money."

"Just tell her what you want her to do," Nick said, "And we can get this over with."

"Just like that, huh? While you two sit around and listen?"

"Well," Sam said. "You can drag it out for hours or you can just tell us what's on your mind."

"What's on my mind is that I need to get out of the country so they don't find out I'm alive. Janice can stay here for a few months and sell the house and then follow me wherever I decide to go. That way it will seem like she is just changing her life."

"Not a bad plan," Sam said. "How are you going to live in this foreign country?"

"Presumably she'll give me some money to live on until she joins me," Tim said.

"How much?" Sam said.

"Oh, a million ought to do it. That way I can buy us a house and get things set up for when she comes."

"Oh, Tim, that sounds like a wonderful idea," Janice said.

"Okay," Sam said, "If that's the plan, we have to run it past Janice's lawyer to see what legal problems it might raise for her. For one thing, if she keeps this money, knowing you are alive, she becomes an accessory to your crime, even though she was not originally a part of it and she also would be committing a crime herself. Now I'm not saying she shouldn't do that, I'm just saying that's what she would be doing if she keeps that money and you are alive. And I'm sure there is other stuff too that I don't know anything about.

That's why she needs to talk to her lawyer."

"That's why she needs to talk to me, not her lawyer. I'm her husband; we'll figure this out together."

"You're a slow learner, Tim," Nick said. "She's going to talk to her lawyer and then she can do whatever she wants."

"Our job, Tim, is not to tell anybody what to do. It is just to make sure that our client knows what she is doing. If she knows what her risks are and she wants to do it anyway, God bless her," Sam said.

Janice squeezed Tim's hand more firmly. "Don't be angry, Tim. We don't have any choice. If I fire them, they will call the police and then there won't be any money because they'll know you're alive."

"So you're strong-armed by the hired help," Tim said, disgustedly.

"Nobody's strong-arming her," Sam said. "If she decides she wants to run away with you and give you all her money, that's her business. We don't care. Our only requirement is that she find out what legal problems she might have if she does that."

"And in the meantime," Nick said, "We have to try to keep her alive."

"Yeah, so now you're the big tough guys who protect my wife from me and everyone else," Tim said.

"The thing is, Tim," Sam said, "I didn't see you here when the two big guys tried to kill her. So Yeah. That's our job."

Tim and Janice went upstairs into the bedroom for two hours and when they came out, Janice was beaming and holding on to Tim's arm.

"I'll see the lawyer tomorrow," Janice said. "So will you come back tomorrow night?"

"I'll be here," Tim said, looking angrily at Sam, who was reading a magazine.

Janice let Tim out the front door and came back hugging herself and smiling. "Oh my God," she said, "He's alive. My husband is alive."

"He certainly is," Sam said.

* * *

"You won't believe what happened," Tim growled into the cell phone. "My wife hired these two goons to protect her and they damned near screwed everything up."

"What do you mean?" Linda asked.

"Well, they're there in the house. They wouldn't even let me get near her. They made me tell her in front of them that I wanted to go to another country and she could give me some money to live on and then she could follow me."

"Why didn't you just tell them to leave? It's your house."

"Because they said if they left, they would call the police."

"Jesus. And she just sat there?"

"Yeah. It seems these guys saved her life. Some contractor is trying to kill her and they saved her."

"What? Why would someone want to kill her?"

"It's the contractor who repaired the bridge. She's suing him because his repairs caused the bridge to collapse and kill me. She somehow found out that he cut a lot of corners, and that's why the bridge collapsed. The government would find that out if she goes ahead with the lawsuit, so he tried to kill her."

"Well, did you get any money out of her?"

"I don't know. I asked her for a million dollars."

"I thought you were going to ask for all of it."

"I couldn't. These two goons were right there and she wouldn't talk about it without them."

"Is she going to give you the million dollars?"

"I don't know. She's going to talk to her lawyer tomorrow."

"Her lawyer. Why in the hell is she talking to her lawyer?"

"That's what the goons insist on. They say they don't care what she does, but she has to talk to the lawyer first so she knows what she's doing."

"Damn. The whole idea is we'd take everything before she knew what happened," Linda said.

"I know. I just had to think on my feet, so I just asked for the million. If we get it, we can still go away," Tim said.

"Yeah," she said, sullenly.

"I'll see you in a little bit," he said.

"Why even bother?" She said. "We're fucked."

"Just wait till I get there, O.K., we'll talk about it then."

Tim got in his Beetle and Nick followed half a block back, watching the signal from the electronic transmitter he had placed under the Beetle's bumper. Half an hour later, Nick saw Tim pull up outside an apartment building in the Shadyside section of the city. He parked and watched.

CHAPTER TWENTY-THREE

"Timeeeeee," Linda slurred, as Tim came through the door. "The return of Boy-Wonder. He may not have the money, but whut the fuck," she trailed off.

She was drunk again. Drunk and belligerent.

"Couldn't you wait until I got home to get drunk?"

"Why should I do that? First of all, yur dead. Second of all, you ain't got the money. Do I need to be sober to deal with that?"

"Haven't got the money," he corrected, hating her ignorance.

Linda took a long pull of cheap wine, burped, and head down, eyes up, said, "Haven't got the money or ain't got the money, honey, you done fucked up."

"What the hell is wrong with you?" Tim said. "We can still get the money, maybe even all of it, but if not all, then probably a million dollars. That's pretty damned good, I'd say."

"Yeahhhhhh," she slurred. "You'd say. But, Tim-eeeeeee, what would I say? I'd say you fucked up and I'd say we ain't got squat."

"Haven't got squat," Tim corrected, gritting his teeth.

"Yehhhhhhh. Whatever."

"Come on," he said, slapping on a cheap wig that came down over his ears and a sticky moustache the same gray color as the wig, "We're going out. I'm not sitting here all night with a drunken bimbo. You're going to eat and sober up." Then Tim grabbed her under the arms and lifted her to a standing position.

"Bimbo," she muttered, "You're a bimbo."

Tim put a jacket on her and held her up as they walked to the elevator. He hoped that the cool night air would wake her up a bit. The couple emerged from the front of the building with Linda leaning on Tim and Tim turning to fix her jacket and kiss her eyes. It was a good profile shot. Nick fired away with the Nikon D2x and its vibration reduction 200mm lens. The light was perfect with the couple standing under the entrance lamps. Each frame was time and date stamped.

Nick followed the hapless couple from restaurant to bar to an outside French bistro where Linda finally seemed to be able to drink her own coffee. Prior to this, Nick had a number of shots of Tim feeding and kissing her.

When Nick returned to Janice's house, it was in the early hours of the morning. He briefly showed Sam some of the shots. "Rough day tomorrow," Sam said.

* * *

Cochran brought bagels for breakfast about eight thirty the next morning. Sam made coffee and Nick got out the cream cheese and jam. Janice came down when the table was set.

Cochran began with, "I don't think there's too much to say about your problem. If you go away with your husband and keep the insurance money, you will be committing insurance fraud, which has a jail sentence of ten to fifteen years."

"Any other hazards?" Nick said.

"I can't think of any except that Janice and Tim would become vulnerable to blackmail. If anyone found out who they are, they could demand money in exchange for not turning them in."

"How safe are they in a foreign country?" Sam asked.

"If you're talking about extradition, I don't know anything about that. Some countries will not extradite a person for certain crimes; others will. You'd have to research that. And, of course, Tim would have to assume a false identity."

"What if Tim were involved with another woman?" Sam said.

"What are you talking about?" Janice spat out.

"What if, right now, Tim is involved in a relationship with another woman?" Sam said.

"What are you trying to do? You just don't like him," Janice cried.

"Show her," Sam said to Nick.

Nick got out a laptop computer and loaded the camera's memory card into the slot. As the machine booted up, he explained.

"I took these shots last night after Tim left. I followed him home," Nick said.

The first image that came on the screen was a picture of Tim Kissing Linda's face under the entrance lights of the apartment building.

"You will notice," Nick said, "That the time and date stamp down in the corner tells you that this picture was taken last night just before ten o'clock."

Janice sat through twenty-five of the pictures before she got up from the table and ran sobbing into her room.

"Big problem I see," Cochran said, "Is the possibility that this new woman must know who he is, and if he leaves her for Janice, she could blackmail them. If he doesn't leave her but wants the money from Janice, there are obvious problems for Janice."

CHAPTER TWENTY-FOUR

When Tim arrived that evening, Janice was curled up on the couch sobbing. Nick checked Tim for weapons, this time without throwing him to the floor, and Sam covered with the shotgun. Ronin watched.

Tim walked into the living room and saw Janice curled up on the couch hugging her legs and trying to hide her red eyes. "What did you do to my wife?" Tim said to no one in particular.

"You'd better go talk to her," Nick said.

Tim walked over and sat next to Janice, putting his hand on her knee. "What's wrong, honey?" He said.

"She's afraid you're going to be mad when you find out what she did," Sam said.

"What?" He said, looking first and Janice and then back to Sam. "What did she do?"

"She gave it back," Nick said.

"Gave it back? Gave what back?" Tim said, visibly panicked.

"She gave back all the money, minus our fee, of course," Sam said. "She gave it all back."

Tim pulled his hand back from Janice's knee as if the knee were a hot stove. He stared open-mouthed first at his wife and then at Sam and Nick.

"She what?" He yelled. "You let her..."

"It was hers, Tim. We couldn't do anything," Sam said.

"Hers? Are you nuts? Hers? It was mine. It was mine," Tim shouted. "Gave it back? What do I do now?"

Janice stopped sobbing and just watched Tim, disbelief in her face. "I don't know you," she said softly with anger.

"You gave it back? You didn't even talk to me. You idiot. You gave it back? What could possibly induce you to do that? Three million dollars? You gave three million dollars away? Why? What about me? What about us? How will we live now? We have nothing. I have nothing. You are completely, utterly, and totally insane," he yelled.

"Is that all you care about," Janice said thinly. "The money? Is that it?"

"Well, there's not much point in anything else without the money, is there?" He glared at her.

"So you came back here for the money and not for me?" She said.

"Of course I came back for the money. Why do you think I stayed hidden. I came back for you too, but without the money, we're finished. I don't have a job. You don't have any money."

"You called me an idiot."

"You are an idiot. First you fill up my house with these muscle-headed bozos and then you give away three million dollars. I'd say you're an idiot. Yes, I would."

"Why does this have to be just about money?" Janice said.

"What else do you suggest?" Tim said.

"How about love?" Janice said.

"How about it? Love on nothing a year. That's good. Real attractive. Good idea."

"You don't seem to have any trouble loving that other woman," Janice said. "The blonde with the short skirt."

Tim looked at Janice, and then at Sam and Nick. "So that's it. You got pissed because of Linda and you decided you would get me, and you threw the money away."

"Yes," Janice said.

"Well, that was stupid. You could have kept most of the money and I could have gone off with Linda. That was really stupid," Tim said. "I could never imagine you would, you could do something that stupid."

"Get out," Janice said, quietly. "Just get out."

Nick let Tim out and watched to make sure he drove off and that no one else was there. Ronin went to Janice and she petted him for a while, then she got up and walked over to Sam, putting her head on his shoulder and sobbing.

CHAPTER TWENTY-FIVE

Wolfgang Badersault could see his breath on the patio in the mornings. Nonetheless, or maybe because of that, he took his coffee outside. He dragged his emaciated frame and his oversized head out to a table and chair with a cushion on it that had been kept inside all night, and he had his coffee. Strong, black, three more cups in the chrome insulated carafe sitting in the middle of the table.

Badersault thought back to stories he had heard his grandfather tell about Buddhist monks. His grandfather was a religious man, a Catholic, but he loved all religions. The story that always stuck with the young Badersault was of the monk who could never achieve enlightenment, but who, one evening, saw his own body floating underneath the footbridge where he stood. That was his enlightenment.

Badersault felt that now. He saw the world around him going on without him. He wasn't necessary for the world. And when he was gone, it would be as if he were never there. That was odd. It seemed to him that everyone thought his particular existence was a matter of extreme importance. Nothing was more important. Nothing was more compelling. Other people even acted that way about others' existence sometimes. Doctors ran around in a rush trying to save someone's life. Why? The world went on one way or another.

Why did all this stuff seem important? Why did it ever seem important? What if he were poor? What would be different? Maybe it was just all a game. You had to do something between birth and death and so you played this game. If you were poor, you would play the poor game. But rich or poor, you were supposed to pretend that things meant something, that it was important who won and who lost. You never really believed it was, but you pretended. Everyone did.

So when it's all said and done, are you, Wolfgang Badersault, just another molecule like all the other molecules? You used to think it made a difference if you had dinner with a president or if senators called you for advice — and money — and if you owned the finest motor cars ever produced and if you gave men jobs and had more money than you needed. But now none of this seemed important.

What difference did any of this make? He was confused. This bridge thing. Why did he agree to let that fool Wysorek short the materials on the bridge? He didn't need the money. It seemed harmless enough at the time. No one would discover that shortages in materials for years, maybe decades. The thing was over-designed. Who the hell would have guessed it would fall down? How was it even possible for it to fall down? What if it had fallen down at rush hour? That's when it should have fallen, with all the weight.

So there's this woman with a dead husband and she wants money. Just like the hookers and his ex-wife and his kids and everyone else he knew. And he's agreed to pay her. Why didn't he just pay her to begin with? Now his one friend, Wally Federman, is in the ground.

And who is this muscle she's got working for her? The guy's good enough to kill Federman. That's pretty damned good. Maybe he should hire this guy to work for him. Yeah, but what for, so he can kill more people? Why does he need to kill any more people?

He dialed the number Sam had given him.

Janice answered.

"Let me talk to the bodyguard," Badersault said.

Sam came on the phone. "This is John Donne."

"This is Wolfgang Badersault. Take the woman to Dangle and Killem sometime today. They will have a release for her to sign and they will transfer money electronically to her account."

"O.K.," Sam said.

"And after that, I'd like you to come to my house," Badersault said.

Sam paused and then said, "I won't be able to do that. I can't protect myself there. You've already said you might decide to kill me. It's possible I would drive in and never be seen again. How about if we meet at the Palomino Restaurant downtown, any time you say?"

"Tonight, seven."

"I'll be there," Sam said.

That afternoon, Sam and Janice went to Dangle and Killem in One Oxford Center, twenty-second floor, downtown. Nick accompanied them into the building and waited in the three story lobby. Better to have eyes in two places. Sam and Nick were able to communicate by headsets. Sam wore a Glock Model 20 chambered in 10mm with a Model 27 chambered in 40 S&W on his ankle. Nick wore a light three quarter length raincoat. Luckily the weather had been unusually cool, 50's during the day and 40's at night, and the coat did not seem unusual. What was unusual was what he had underneath. A FN PS90, a short rifle in bullpup configuration chambered in 5.7 x 28 with a standard fifty round magazine. It was slung under his shoulder like a short yardstick.

In the elevator, Janice stepped over to Sam and straightened his tie. It was a wifely thing to do. Then she took his arm. Another wifely thing. Then she moved closer so that her thigh was touching him. Then the elevator door opened onto a large waiting room. The room was thirty feet square, carpeted from wall to wall with a light green wool carpet, and in the middle of the room, an antique Farahan Persian carpet. Ahead of them were floor-to-ceiling windows displaying the city far below. Ahead of the windows was an elaborate curving desk made of exotic wood with an exotic blonde sitting behind it. Her hair was picked up in a beehive and the hairdo seemed to accentuate the strong lovely features of her oval face. She smiled as they approached her desk.

"Can I help you?" Linda said.

"We're here to see Mr. Delay. Sam Budda and Janice Brannigan."

"Yes, Mr. Delay asked me to escort you to the conference room. He'll be right there."

The woman at the desk was only in her early thirties, but her face was a little puffy, and up close, her lipstick was too thick and too bright. Her eyes were heavily made up and so it was hard to tell what they were like, but the general effect, Sam thought, was beauty in premature decay.

They followed Linda down the hall and around two corners to a large conference room with a large conference table.

"Sit anywhere. Mr. Delay will be right in. Can I get you anything?" Linda asked.

"No, thank you," Janice said, icily.

"I guess you didn't like her," Sam said.

"No, but you obviously did," Janice said.

"I did?"

"I saw the way you looked at her."

"Nice body," Sam said. "Little too much make up, though."

"Hummph," Janice offered.

A trim thirty-five year old came in the conference room, offering his outstretched hand to whomever would grasp it.

"I'm Clarence Delay," he said. "Nice to meet you both."

"I'm John Donne and this is Janice Brannigan," Sam said.

"Please sit," Delay said. He opened a folder and took out a release form.

"If you'll sign this, I'll get it notarized and then I'll call Mellon Bank and authorize the transfer of the funds."

"I'll need to fax this to our attorney," Sam said.

"No need," Delay said. "Mr. Badersault instructed me to use the release you gave him. I advised him to change it so that it was not so one-sided, but he refused my advice, so you'll be signing your own release."

Sam and Janice read the release and confirmed it was the same. Janice signed. Delay was about to leave the room with the release to get it notarized, but Sam insisted that he remain in the room and have the notary come there. He did. When the document was notarized and Janice was given a copy, Delay called the bank on the speaker phone and authorized the transfer of three million dollars from Badersault's account into Janice's. The bank confirmed and gave Janice a transaction number. She then called her personal banker, who confirmed that three million dollars had been transferred to her account under the transaction number she recited.

Delay walked them out to the reception area and shook hands with both. The blonde smiled at Sam and he smiled back. In the elevator, Janice grabbed Sam by the collar of his jacket and kissed him, throwing her arms around his neck.

"I'm rich now," she said.

"You were rich before," he said.

"You did this for me," she said. "I owe you."

She kept her arms around his neck and pressed her breasts into his chest. The bell rang surprisingly fast, and they were on the ground floor. She stepped away, facing the doors, and the doors opened. Nick sat across the lobby, watching.

Sam took Janice by the arm and hustled her outside to the Lincoln Town Car limousine they had hired. Nick covered them while they got in the car. Nick followed in a second Lincoln Town Car limousine.

When they were under way, Janice slid across the seat, reached across and pulled Sam toward her. She kissed him again.

"I think we need to discuss this a bit," Sam said. "I don't get involved with the people I work for. It may not seem a big thing to you, but it can get you killed."

"Maybe I should fire you," she said. "I don't want you killed."

CHAPTER TWENTY-SIX

The Palomino Restaurant was located on the first floor of an office tower near the Point in downtown Pittsburgh. Sam and Nick watched the building from different angles and communicated through their headsets. Badersault had arrived accompanied by four bodyguards. Two were in the restaurant, two were in the lobby of the office tower in which the restaurant was located. The lobby was the only entrance to the restaurant.

Guessing that the two in the lobby were going to brace him for weapons, Sam found the kitchen entrance and, over numerous objections, went into the dining room that way.

Badersault was sitting next to a twelve foot window looking out over a patio. The bodyguards saw Sam first. They glanced at the lobby, then back to Sam, who was nearing the table where Badersault sat, facing Sam. As they moved to intercept Sam, Sam pointed his finger at them and looked at Badersault. Badersault looked up and waved them off. Sam sat.

Badersault wore a blue wool custom-made suit, white shirt, and a patterned tie. A white gold Blancpain wristwatch showed slightly at his wrist. Sam also wore a blue suit. It was an off the rack Hickey Freeman, a starched white shirt and a striped lavender and blue tie. The suit was cut to conceal two guns.

"I don't want to get off on the wrong foot, here, Mr. Badersault, but it's bad manners to brace me with bodyguards after you have invited me to dinner," Sam said.

"Just a precaution," Badersault said.

"One you don't need to take," Sam said. "You just paid my client three million dollars. I am not likely to pose any threat to you. You simply wanted to show me that you're in charge. You're not."

"Pretty aggressive, aren't you?"

"Don't fuck with me. I'm not one of your employees," Sam said.

"Your attitude can get you in trouble, Mr. Donne."

"My attitude is fine, Mr. Badersault. Your problem is that you're used to having people fall down and grovel. You think that's normal. I'll fall down if you shoot me, but I won't grovel."

"Pride goeth before the fall," Badersault said.

"Ditto," Sam said.

"I didn't ask you here to fight with you," Badersault said.

"Why did you ask me here?" Sam said.

The waiter came. Sam ordered the oversized scallops and a Caesar salad. Badersault ordered Alaskan Salmon and the Caesar salad.

"I asked you here to learn who you are."

"Why should I want you to know who I am?" Sam asked.

"It might be worth it," Badersault said.

"How?"

"I'm a very wealthy man. I may want to offer you work."

"With respect, Mr. Badersault, you don't need to hire me. You are surrounded by bodyguards who seem to be pretty good at what they do."

"I know that. But they're not very interesting. They're muscles and guns and nothing more."

"You want interesting?" Sam said.

"Yes."

"Well, no one has ever accused me of being interesting," Sam said.

"I think you're interesting," Badersault said. "You got three million out of me and you killed a man who was very close to me and who was hard to kill."

"The three million was only fair, and you saw that, so you paid it. As for your man, I would rather not have killed him. He left us no choice."

"Us?"

"I work with a partner," Sam said.

"Did you kill my man, or did your partner?"

"I won't discuss that."

"Why won't you tell me?"

"What difference does it make?"

"I'd like to know how he died."

"He died after he nearly killed my hundred and fifty pound guard dog and after he knocked me to the ground with the hardest punch I've ever taken. He was shot with two rounds of double ought buck to the head at point blank range and there was some question whether that would stop him."

"Well, at least that sounds like Federman," Badersault said.

"It wasn't smart going after Mrs. Brannigan," Sam said.

"I didn't order it. I told them to stay away from her. I didn't want the bad press. The nigger did it on his own. Federman did what the nigger told him. That was his one shortcoming," Badersault said.

"That kind of bad judgment can come back on you."

"Don't I know it. That's one of the reasons I paid your lady friend. I figured she'd really be after my ass since my men tried to kill her."

"At least you're honest about it," Sam said.

"I like to surround myself with people who know what they're doing."

"Really," Sam said. "I'd say that hasn't worked out too well with the guy who fixed that bridge for you or the guys who tried to kill Mrs. Brannigan."

"That's my point," Badersault said. "It's hard to find people I can trust. I was hoping you would consider coming to work for me. I have a feeling I could trust you."

"Are you a watch collector?" Sam said.

"What? No. Why?"

"That watch you're wearing is a Blancpain Concept half-hunter triple-date with a moon phase made of white gold with a thirty jewel handmade movement. It has a hundred hours of power reserve," Sam said.

Badersault looked at the watch and then at Sam. "Amazing," he said. "You know more about this watch than I do."

"My guess is that you hired somebody to advise you on watches just like you're trying to hire me. The guy did a pretty good job too."

"It's a good watch?"

"Yeah. It's a good watch, but more than that, your advisor had your number. This watch is known in the trade as "Napoleon I." That fits, doesn't it?"

"Why do they call it that?" Badersault said, testily.

"Because Napoleon commissioned such a watch from Blancpain. It was to be robust and protected. Hence the hunter case," Sam said.

"I paid twenty grand. Did I get my money's worth?"

"No question about it. It's worth about $25,000 and it's a better watch than most. So yeah, you got your money's worth."

"You're making my point for me. It pays to hire the best people. And I think you would enjoy working in my operation."

"I appreciate the offer, Mr. Badersault. I really do. But it wouldn't work. I don't take orders very well and I don't really relate to money. You and I would disagree."

"What do you mean you don't relate to money? You took me for three million dollars."

"That was for my client. Her husband was killed. You killed him. She needed money."

"From what I hear, she already had three million dollars from the insurance companies. Why did she need any more than that?" Badersault said.

"Who can put a price on the loss of a husband or wife?" Sam said.

Badersault toyed with his salad. He ate the rough equivalent of one forkful and pushed it away.

"I want to do something different with the rest of my life," Badersault said.

"And?" Sam asked.

"And nothing," Badersault said. "I thought you might want to be along for the ride."

"One thing I noticed in this business," Sam said. "Tigers don't change their stripes."

"What?"

"You're sitting here in a fancy restaurant surrounded by hired thugs, wearing a five thousand dollar suit and a twenty-five thousand dollar watch telling me you're going to change your life."

"Are you any different?"

"Maybe not, but I'm not offering you a job working for the newer better me," Sam said.

The giant scallops were delicious. Badersault picked at his salmon.

CHAPTER TWENTY-SEVEN

Sam and Nick talked about Badersault's proposal on the way home. Neither were interested in selling their soul to that particular devil. Janice was left in the company of Ronin. There was no longer a reason to be concerned about an attack by Badersault. In fact, since the money had been paid, the new arrangement was that either Sam or Nick would stay at Janice's house all night. The other could sleep in his own bed. Tonight it was Sam's turn to stay with Janice.

They both checked the house and made sure that none of the various silent alarms had been tripped. None had. Janice was fine. Nick went home.

Sam had settled down with Ronin in the living room to read an article on the 5.7 x 28 round for the FN rifle when Janice came out in her bathrobe to ask if she could get him anything.

"No thanks, I'm fine," Sam said, looking over the top of his magazine.

Janice came in the living room, stood in front of Sam, unbelted her robe, and let it fall on the floor. She had on a short negligee that barely reached her thighs. She stood provocatively, with one leg forward and played with Sam's shoe with her toes.

"You sure I can't get you anything?" She said.

Sam's cock started to rise. He crossed his legs and said, "Janice, I told you. I don't get involved with clients. You're very attractive and I'd like nothing better, but I can't do this."

She stepped toward him and uncrossed his legs and then sat down on his lap. Then she reached down and felt his hard cock.

"Not interested, huh?" She smiled.

She then pushed forward so that her bush was rubbing his cock, and she leaned back braced on his knees, her nipples erect through the negligee, her head thrown back, her hair loose and flowing behind her.

"Janice, please," Sam said.

She raised her head and looked at him playfully. "You don't like it that way?" She said.

Deftly, she backed off his lap, stood in front of him, turned around, lifted her negligee above her hips, and backed up with her ass against his chest and her hands on his knees. "You like it from the back?" She turned her head.

He grabbed her to keep her from falling, holding on to her waist, the melons of her ass rubbing gently against his shirt, the lips of her pussy moist, inviting.

"Janice, you've got to stop. Please, I can't do this," he said.

Again, Janice got up, pulled her negligee completely over her head, and stepped toward him completely naked. Again, she mounted him, straddling his legs, and this time she brushed her nipples against his face, turning side to side. Sam laughed and tried to steady her so she wouldn't fall.

"Janice, Please," he pleaded.

"Be careful or I'll hurt you with one of these," she said.

"I know you will," he laughed. "Please, please stop it. You're very attractive and you can see how my body is reacting, but I can't do this. It's nothing to do with you. You're very desirable, but this is something I can't do."

She stopped, sat back on his lap, naked, and looked at him.

"I know you're not gay," she said.

"Yeah, you can tell that," he said.

"Then what is it?"

"It's two things. One thing is I'm involved with a woman already, and the other is what I've been telling you. If I let myself do this, I will end up dead. Maybe not tonight, but some night. And that's stupid."

"Who is the woman? Your wife?"

"No."

"Is she pretty?"

"I think so."

"Do you love her?"

"That's a little too personal."

"Well, I'm sitting here on your lap naked. That's pretty personal, isn't it?"

"Yeah, it is."

"Then do you love her?"

"That's too personal."

Janice got off Sam's lap, bent down, swept her robe off the floor, put it on, and walked out of the room. There were tears in her eyes.

At two o'clock, Sam checked the monitors and the infra red sensors and the silent tripwires. Everything was O.K.

At least it was O.K. outside, but it wasn't O.K. inside his head. He almost lost it earlier. What a moron. He should have shut her down before it ever got to that. He was incompetent. Maybe he was just too old for this work. He wasn't good at it any more. Show him a naked woman and his training, his will to survive, his control, his dedication, his skill, his discipline just evaporated.

It was midnight Albuquerque time, and he dialed Maria.

She answered, sleepy.

"Maria, it's me, Sam," he said.

"Oh, Sam. I'm so glad you called. I've been thinking about you."

"I've been thinking about you too," he said.

"How's it going there?" She said.

"Pretty well. I got the client a three million dollar settlement for her lawsuit," he said.

"Jesus, how'd you do that?"

"Well, he sent two guys to kill her and one of them ended up dead, so he thought it might be better to pay."

"Still, that's pretty unusual," she said.

"It is, but this guy's got so much money that he literally won't miss it, and it gets him out from under a lot of bad publicity," Sam said.

"Why does he care?"

"Because he wants the next bridge repair job where he'll rip off the state again and make probably twice as much as he paid the client."

"Oh, so it comes down to money," she said.

"Yeah, doesn't it always," he said. "Actually, the guy's real smart. He repairs the bridge so badly that it falls down and he rakes in a bundle for all the materials he shorted them. Then he bids for the contract to clean up the mess he created and also the contract to do the second repair job."

"Does he have a prayer of getting these other contracts?" She said.

"Oh yeah, as long as the publicity about the bridge that collapsed isn't too bad," he said.

"So, how's your sex life?" She said.

"Pretty inactive, except the client's been hitting on me. How's yours," he said.

"Same, except I don't have a client. Did you fuck her?"

"No, but the thought crossed my mind."

"Why didn't you?"

"I don't get involved with clients."

"Is that it?"

"Pretty much, except she's a blonde and I've been looking for an attractive dark haired woman with a big nose," he said.

"Big nose?" She snorted.

"Yeah. Know any?"

"No. I hear most of those women live in Albuquerque."

"I'll have to check it out after I finish here," he said.

"I'll be here," she said.

CHAPTER TWENTY-EIGHT

Badersault sat in his library. It was a large room with twenty foot ceilings and windows with panes all along the outside wall. The inside walls were lined with bookshelves going from the floor up fifteen feet. The bookcases were wooden and the books were leather-bound. Badersault never read any of them, but he had spent more than three hundred thousand dollars buying them with the advice of a bookseller in New York. The room was forty by thirty and had a massive fireplace on the long interior wall, which was blazing away on this chilly summer evening.

Badersault was on a large leather couch facing the fire, and he was flanked by two massive leather wing back chairs. Between the chairs and in front of the couch was a rainbow Senna, an antique Persian carpet. Behind the couch was a long library table, almost like a conference table, with chairs at intervals along its length.

After the fire had died down a bit, there was a knock. The man servant entered and said that Mr. Morengeone was outside.

"Send him in," Badersault said.

Morengeone came into the room. His wrist was bandaged and there was a lump on his shoulder where a bandage had been placed under his shirt. The folds of his face glistened and stubble bristled as it usually did. His bloodshot eyes widened at the aspect of the room. He had never been in the house before. He held a cap in his hand.

"Sit down, Bartholomew," Badersault said, motioning to one of the large chairs.

Morengeone smiled, revealing the yellow canines. "Some crib," he said, sitting.

"Wysorek tells me you fucked up," Badersault said.

Morengeone's toothy smile evaporated and his expression hardened. "What you mean?" He said.

"You went after the Brannigan woman when he told you not to," Badersault said.

"Yeah, he tole me that, but I knew it couldn't be right. He's just a fat fuck don't know which end's up," Morengeone said. "The bitch was part of the problem. She was suin you. And she was right there where I thought I could get at her."

"But you were wrong, weren't you," Badersault said.

"I didn't have no way to know about them two crackers and that big fuckin dog."

"Well, that's the point, my man. It was your business to know about that, and you fucked up. If they were there, it was your job to know it."

Morengeone looked uncomfortable and irritated.

"I don't pay you to fuck up. I pay you to get results. You hear me?"

"Yeah, I hear you."

"Now what I need to know is this. I got some other work that needs to be done, but I need to have it done by someone who can follow orders. Can you do that?"

"I can do that. I just gots to know what the orders is."

"From now on, you deal with me," Badersault said, "And I'll give you the orders."

"That's better. The fat man, Wysorek, he and me we don't get along too good."

"You don't have to worry about that any more. Here's my problem," Badersault said. "I want that new bridge contract, but I won't get it if there is any bad publicity about the last job I did."

"Yee, and that bitch, she be rasin a stink," Morengeone said.

"Leave her out of this. She's not your concern. I paid her off. She withdrew the suit. But that PennDOT guy may still cause trouble and that guy who used to work for us, the one you chased, he may cause trouble too."

"So you want them taken care of?" Bartholomew said.

"Yes. Both of them. The PennDOT guy is easy to find. You can just kill him in his house. The other guy, I understand, has disappeared. I'd like you to watch the Brannigan broad's house to see if he turns up there. He probably will. They'll think the heat is off now that the lawsuit is over so they won't be looking for anyone watching."

"You want me to jack up that bitch?"

"No."

"What about them guys with her?"

"Leave them alone."

"So you just want me to ice the PennDOT guy and Jimmy Reynolds?"

"Yeah."

"I may need some help. My wrist ain't right yet."

"Got anyone in mind?"

"Yeah, a guy I worked with before."

"Who is he?"

"His name Alphonse Whipdick."

"You got to be kidding," Badersault said.

"No, I not. He can kill a man with his cock."

Badersault snickered.

"I'll probably need another man too. Joe Bob Smith. He a fine killer. Word is he killed his momma for two shots and a beer."

"O.K.," Badersault said. "Bring 'em on, but keep 'em on a short leash. I don't want no stone killers runnin around rapin' and pillagin' on my dime."

"No sir. Mr. Count. I be watchin' 'em. And we leave the rapin' and pillagin' to you."

Badersault looked up, a slight smile on his face. It seemed that Bartholomew was capable of a bit of humor.

CHAPTER TWENTY-NINE

This time Tim didn't call Linda. He didn't think he could face her scorn when he told her Janice had given back the money. Tension had been building between them because of the delay in getting paid and the reduced amount of the payment. Now, if he told her there was no money at all, she would go ballistic. If she was drunk when he got there, so much the better.

"Hi," she said when he opened the door. She wasn't drunk.

"Hi," he said.

"Well, how'd it go? Did we get the million?"

Tim said nothing and pushed past her into the living room. He sat on the couch looking disheveled.

"What's the matter? Did you get it? Did you get the money?"

"No. We didn't," he said, dejected. "I need a drink."

"Why the hell not?" She said, raising her voice. Her face flashed anger. She stood aside as Tim brushed past her again on the way to the bar. She stared after him and folded her arms across her chest in a gesture of last-straw disbelief. Her lips were tightly pursed and the color in her face was starting to rise.

Ice clinked in a glass and Tim poured some of Linda's bourbon in it. He took a swallow and said, "Because one of her bodyguards followed me home and saw us together that night. And they told her about it."

"That's it?" She said.

"No that's not it. She was so pissed off about you that she gave the money back to the insurance company," he said.

Linda's mouth dropped. "She what?"

"She gave it back."

"Three million dollars?"

"Yeah. That's what I said," Tim said.

"I don't believe it," she said. "How do you know?"

"She told me. The bodyguard told me."

"And you just believed them, like a big dope."

"Face it Linda. There's no money. We screwed up. You're a drunk and I'm a fuck up."

"I'm no drunk, you loser," she said.

"Loser? I wasn't a loser when you couldn't get enough of me."

"Yeah, that was when you had some money. Now you're just nothin."

"So I'm 'nothin' and you turn out to be a drunk bimbo," Tim said, taking another stiff drink.

"You can't call me a bimbo, you loser. I got a job. They like me there. I do important stuff. I work with important people. Until you came around, I had money."

"Yeah, real important," he huffed. "A fucking secretary."

"Well, I was good enough to fuck you, I guess," she said, standing over him, hands on hips.

"Whatever," he said, taking another drink.

"Yeah, whatever. Well, what are you going to do now, big shot? Start goin to the welfare office?"

Tim was on his second big glass of bourbon by now and he was drunk. "Is that all it is with you, Linda, is that all it is, money?"

"No. That's all it is with you. That's all it ever was. You couldn't leave your wife because of money. It would cost too much. Now you pretend you're dead. Why? Because of money. But your wife is too smart for you. She knows how to hurt you. She gives it all back."

"You only fucked me because I had money," Tim slurred. "You said so yourself. You're all bitches."

"And you're a loser," she said, walking away.

CHAPTER THIRTY

Morengeone recruited two assistants, Alphonse Whipdick and Joe Bob Smith, both experienced killers and sociopaths who had worked with him before. They were staying on the Badersault estate in the gardener's quarters until Morengeone could find them a more suitable place in Pittsburgh. For the last two days, they had been playing poker, and they were beginning to get on each other's nerves.

Alphonse Whipdick sat at a table in the gardener's outbuilding dealing a game of five card draw. Joe Bob Smith sat across from him and picked up the cards as Whipdick dealt them. Whipdick was an American Indian of unknown origin. He wore a red bandana tied around his head with his long, shiny black hair hanging straight down. He was of ordinary build, trim, in his thirties, and his face was creased and weathered. He had the profile of the classic Indian warrior. His dark eyes moved slowly, almost cautiously, on each side of his hawk nose and he never smiled.

Joe Bob Smith, on the other hand, was a West Virginia boy. He was emaciated. No one could tell his age. It could have been twenty or it could have been fifty. Or maybe he was sixty. The skin was stretched tight on his face, almost as if he were dead and the fluids had evaporated from his body, leaving only the skin taut against his bones. His cheeks were especially prominent, and his blue eyes stared with fixed attention from holes surrounded by puckered skin. He was five-ten and weighed a hundred forty pounds, but that was only when he was dressed in his steel toed shoes and three sweaters. He smoked without interruption and was always cold. His hair was a fringe around the sides and back of his head. A Camel cigarette dangled from his thin lips. His nickname was Juicy Fruit.

"Why they call you Whipdick?" Joe Bob drawled, taking two cards and sucking in smoke from a Camel.

"It's my name," the Indian said.

"That's purely unfortunate," Joe Bob said, blowing smoke out his nose as he pulled a card from the middle of the fan of cards and placing it on the end. "I guess you must'a got whipped by your own dick," he guffawed. "Haw, Haw, Haw," trailing off into coughing and hacking.

"Queens over eights," the Indian said.

"Fuck you," Joe Bob said, throwing his cards in the middle of the table.

"Your deal," the Indian said.

"Wha'd yew like best to do, when yer not cheatin at cards?" Joe Bob drawled, shuffling.

Whipdick thought for a while and then he said, "I like to kill white men."

Joe Bob stopped shuffling, looked at Whipdick, started shuffling again, and said, "Well, ah'l be a motherfucker," the blue eyes inside his dead face flashing at the Indian.

"Yeah," the Indian muttered, moving his cards around in his hand, "Most you scrawny crackers fuck your mothers, I hear."

"You'd prably have trouble hearing without no ears," Joe Bob glowered, dragging on his cigarette and blowing the smoke in Whipdick's direction.

"Why they call you Juicy Fruit? You look like you all dried up," Whipdick said. "You about as juicy as a sand dune. Haw. Haw. Haw. Sand dune."

"Ah ain't no sand dune, Shit Stain," Joe Bob said.

"You dry as a dead rat, been layin in the sun all week," Whipdick smirked.

"You know, Injun, Ahm pretty damned good with a Bowie. I could split you top to bottom jest lak an Injun banana," Joe Bob drawled.

"Ah'l take three cards, dust bin."

"Take these, Moose fart."

" White men. I kill em slow. Poke out an eye. Cut off their lips. Finely, after several hours, I run outa things to cut off and they usuly just die. Most of 'em whimpering for their mommas," Whipdick said.

"Ah hope you ain't got no ahdeahs bout killin me, cause ahl carve your worthless half-breed ass into strip steaks," Joe Bob said.

The Indian picked up his cards.

"I'd scalp you, but somebody beat me to it," the Indian said, looking mischievously over his cards, then breaking out into a loud belly laugh.

"Just play them cards, half-breed."

"Maybe I can still get that little part around the side," the Indian said, breaking out into another belly laugh.

"Just keep at it Geronimo."

"Yeah, but it would be hard to hang that little bit of hair on my belt. It would fall off and the dogs would eat it." Another belly laugh.

" I'm takin' one card," Joe Bod said.

"I'd kill you, white man, but you look like you already dead. It's bad luck to kill a dead man. I bet you sleep in a coffin," the Indian said. "Give me three cards, White Face of Death."

"Here you go you renegade motherfucker. Three cards. How come they ain't strung you up?"

The Indian picked up his cards.

"Ain't no white man can do it," the Indian smiled.

"Ah can do it. Ahl promise you that, you murderin dogshit."

"Let's see what you got, Foxturd," the Indian said.

"Two aces," Joe Bob said.

"Three threes," the Indian said.

"Sonofabitch. Deal the cards," Joe Bob said. "You sure yur name ain't Zipperdick?"

"You loco, white man."

"Yeah, ah loco, but ah think you got yur dick caught in a zipper. That's why they call you Zipperdick."

"I tell you why they call me Whipdick, White Devil. I whipped a man to death with my dick so bad his momma didn't know who it was. And he was a little bastard about your size. White motherfucker, just like you."

"Wal, that's the dumbest thing ah ever hear of. Whip a man to death with yer dick. My ass," Joe Bob snorted, blowing smoke out his nose.

"Not only that, Mousefart, but when I sling my dick up over my shoulder and come down hard, it lop off what was the white bastard's head. The head went rolling down the sidewalk, and his momma, she runnin after it yellin, "Mah boy, Mah boy," Whipdick sneered, arranging his cards.

"Ah take it back," Joe Bob said, "Now that whut you just said was the dumbest thing ah ever heard. The momma yellin "Mah boy, Mah boy," and chasin the head down the street, and you standin there with yer dick over yer shoulder. That's pure fuckin dumb."

"That's the trouble with white men," Alphonse said, sitting back in his chair. "They don't know wisdom from a shriveled dick."

"Ah thank whut musta happened is you shit yer pants, and you gone loco from the stink," Joe Bob said.

Whipdick fingered the cards smoothly and dealt with expertise.

"I never ate me no blue eyes. You wanna pluck one out for me, Deathface, or maybe I just snap it right outa your head and eat it." He grinned.

Instantly, the table was upended and Joe Bob had a nine inch Bowie at Whipdick's throat. Whipdick had a Kelteck .380 at Joe Bob's left eye.

The two men stood tense and poised to kill each other as the door burst open. Morengeone, hearing the yelling, the table being tipped over and glasses crashing on the floor, exploded through the door. "What the fuck," Morengeone yelled, "I cain't leave you two fuckers alone for five minutes witout you goin apeshit."

"Back off nigger, Ahm gonna kill me a half-breed," Joe Bob said.

"Stand back Sambo, this eye's gonna blow right out the back of his head," Whipdick hissed.

Morengeone walked over to the two antagonists and gently pulled the knife and the gun down simultaneously.

"The idea, motherfuckers," he whispered, "Is we kill other people, not ourselves."

CHAPTER THIRTY-ONE

Two months after the collapse of the Liberty Bridge, Wolfgang Badersault met with Pennsylvania Governor J. Percy Fraudmore. At the meeting, two contracts for work on the collapsed Liberty Bridge were awarded to Badersault. Following the signing of the contract, the governor and Badersault conducted a press conference. The governor announced the awarding of the contracts and gave a resounding endorsement of the contractor's work, his employment of union labor, his patriotism, his devotion to his aged mother, and his dedication to equal opportunity.

Badersault stood beaming on the podium with Fraudmore, his outsized head bobbing like a cork on water at each compliment the governor threw his way. He was dressed in one of his five thousand dollar suits with a white shirt and tie, but over the suit he wore a blaze yellow construction vest and a hard hat. He was Mr. Construction. He was the working man in a suit.

The governor himself had gone to pudge the way many middle aged politicians do. His face was puffed up, his hair was oily and slicked back, and his belly bumped repeatedly against the podium. One could see the remnants of a handsome face. Once he was a young man full of promise, a graduate of a fancy school, brimming with energy and anxious ambition all mixed up together. He would talk endlessly about fixing what was broken and making life wonderful for everyone. That was long ago. Now he was a greed machine that sucked up money from any and every crevice.

Fraudmore's friendship with Badersault was longstanding. It went back to his days in the General Assembly when he served on the transportation committee and discovered the allure of envelopes full of twenty dollar bills. Badersault's twenty dollar bills. Fraudmore was distinguished in the General Assembly in that he made the list of the thirteen most corrupt politicians in Pennsylvania every year for fifteen years without a break. He had gone from a dedication to making life better for the masses to making life richer for himself. He was, of course, widely admired, and was elected governor without much opposition.

Badersault, over the years, had watched politicians and had noticed that the most corrupt were often most beloved by the voters. This was true even during the periodic clamors over cleaning up the corruption. The voters were a herd. They seemed to have no collective will.

Badersault considered other herds. It amazed him that the Jews didn't attack their Nazi captors in the concentration camps. Sure, they were emaciated and exhausted from starvation, cold and the work, but why not attack since they outnumbered the guards by huge margins?

Why do hostages relate to their captors? Isn't it the same thing? Badersault developed a theory. It had two parts. The first part was that people adjust to anything. He could destroy the most beautiful woodland in Pennsylvania and replace it with a concrete block shopping mall that itself collapsed within a few years, and people got used to it.

The second part of Badersault's theory was that you could do really bad things to people — and have them accept it — if you made them feel that their life would go on at the same time you were screwing them. Then the threat really wasn't there. For example, Badersault took a little money, but that was no big thing in the whole scheme of things, because the roads still carried the cars, people still went to work, life went on.

"Mr. Badersault," a reporter from the Tribune yelled, "Mr. Badersault."

"Yes," Badersault beamed.

"Sir, I was wondering how you could have the nerve to take the fifteen million dollar contract to clean up and rebuild the bridge after it was your work that caused it to fall down?"

"Well, that's an exaggeration, wouldn't you say?" Badersault said. "That bridge fell down on its own, not because of anything my men did to it."

"But isn't that the point," the reporter persisted. "You were supposed to prevent that from happening. You were supposed to fix the bridge, keep it from falling down. That's why they paid you four million dollars."

Badersault continued smiling, took off his construction helmet, and rubbed his brow, his head bobbing on the emaciated frame. "We did the work they paid us for," he said. "Some things just can't be helped. Next question."

"Mr. Badersault," another reporter said, "How do we know the bridge won't fall down again?"

"We don't," Badersault said, "But you can bet your bottom dollar that the engineers and architects are going to be really careful in their design this time."

"Are you saying it was a design error and not your work that caused the bridge to fail?" A third reporter asked.

"I'm not blaming anyone," Badersault said, "The important thing is that this project is going to employ more than five hundred union working men and when they are through with their skilled work, the city will again have a bridge that will serve it well."

"Thank you," the governor said. "That's all we have time for now. Thank you for coming."

The press continued to clamor and shout, but the two men walked off the podium, talking amiably with each other, surrounded by state policemen, as if no one else were in the room.

"I guess I pulled your ass outa that fire, huh, Wolfgang?" The governor whispered in Badersault's ear.

"Oh, hell, Percy," Badersault said. "You could have let them go on all day. As long as I didn't come right out and say I was robbing the public treasury, it didn't really make any difference what I said. You still gonna use my plane this weekend?"

"Yeah, if it's still available," Fraudmore said.

"Hell, yeah. Anything for a paying customer," Badersault said.

As the two men emerged from the Capitol Building, they paused for photos, beaming and shaking each other's hands. Photographers climbed over each other to get into position for a shot and flashes popped all over the crowd of reporters and photographers. The reporters were still shouting questions and raising their hands to get attention.

Still smiling and hanging onto Badersault's hand, Fraudmore leaned over to Badersault and said, "What a bunch of rubes."

* * *

On the day of the news conference and for several days following, major newspapers across the state carried stories about the fifteen million dollar contract to clean up and repair the Liberty Bridge in Pittsburgh. Some articles commented on the expertise of the Badersault Company in bridge repair; others blamed PennDOT for the collapse of the bridge; others dwelt on the number of people who would be employed on the project; others felt that Pittsburgh was getting more than its share of the state budget; some noted the close friendship between the governor and Wolfgang "the Count" von Badersault.

Only one editorial writer commented that it was odd for the contractor who failed once before, at a cost of millions of dollars, to repair the bridge, to be awarded another contract, three times as big as the first, to do it all over again. Not even that writer, however, came right out and blamed Badersault for the collapse of the bridge, although he did mention what no one else had discovered: that a PennDOT employee had filed a federal lawsuit claiming that Badersault made bad repairs on the Liberty Bridge.

A few days later, on the obituaries page, there was a small article on Henry Blinkman:

> Henry James Blinkman, 49, of Oakmont, was found dead at his home yesterday, an apparent homicide. Police would

not release details on the crime except to say that he was pronounced dead at the scene.

Blinkman had been employed for twenty-six years for PennDOT. He was the supervisor of inspection services and worked on all the major projects in the Pittsburgh area. He is survived by a sister in Seattle.

CHAPTER THIRTY-TWO

The day had started out normally for Henry Blinkman. He was off for three days and he had decided to stay in bed longer than usual. It was, after all, a vacation day. About ten o'clock, he padded out to the kitchen and put on a pot of coffee. As the Mr. Coffee machine burbled and sputtered at the end of its cycle, there was a knock at the front door.

Unusual, Blinkman thought. Who the hell can that be?

He opened the door and looked in the face of Bartholomew Morengeone. The folds of black skin glistened in the morning light, the nose was flat, the mouth wide, smiling, the yellow canines casting a dull and threatening gleam, the bloodshot eyes peering out from under the bill of a cap that said "Plumber."

"I be the plumber," Morengeone said.

"Plumber?" Blinkman said. "I didn't call a plumber."

"Well, hell no. I know you didn't call no plumber. I be here to plumb you up for free. You don't gotta call me."

"Is this some kind of joke?"

"I be a serious motherfucker," Morengeone grinned. "See, I gots pliers and everything." He opened his bag and displayed an assortment of tools. "Ain't no joke."

"I'm afraid you've got the wrong house," Blinkman said.

"You Henry Blinkman, ain't you?"

"Yes, but I don't know you. And I don't know what you're doing here."

"Course you don't, Henry. You gots to plumb you imagination for a reason I be here. It don't jest come right out and fuckin hit you between the eyes wit' it. That why you need a plumber. To help you plumb."

Blinkman tried to close the door. This guy was nuts and he had a crazy look on his face. But Morengeone easily pushed the door open and stepped in, dropping his tool bag and grabbing Blinkman by the robe.

Morengeone kicked the tool bag inside and closed the front door behind him.

"What do you want? I don't have much money. You can have whatever is here. I don't keep money at home. You can have my credit cards," Blinkman stammered, shrinking under the powerful grip of Morengeone .

"I don't have no truck with credit cards, Henry. You a dummy. We off the books now."

"What do you mean 'off the books'? Who are you? What do you want?"

"Henry, goddam it, I tole you, you need help plumbin and I here to help. You need to listen better, motherfucker. It not good to ignore what people say."

"Look, you can have whatever you want. Just take it and leave."

"Henry, Henry, when you havin trouble plumbin you imagination, all that mean is that you all plugged up. Now admit it. You been havin trouble on the crapper, ain't you?"

"What do you mean?"

"You know. It not be comin out. You know, the number two. You prably be sittin there gruntin and groanin and ain't nothin showin up."

"I don't know what you mean."

"Goddam it Henry, I be talking about you on the shitter. You know. You be tryin to shit and the shit it just ain't cooperatin. Ain't no shit in the water."

"You mean I'm constipated."

"Goddam it yes, Henry. That's the fuckin word. I knew you knew it. You contemplated. But the plumber here now, and you don't gots to worry no more."

"What are you talking about?" Henry said, sweating profusely now.

"Well, I fix it for you Henry. After I get through, the shit be flowin through you like a bullet through a gun. Damn, I get through with you, Henry, you be one slick motherfucker. You be a shittin fool."

Blinkman, now thoroughly alarmed, twisted out of Morengeone 's grip and stumbled toward the kitchen and the freedom of the back door. Morengeone caught him, however, grabbing him by the bathrobe. Blinkman, operating on adrenaline, twisted out of the robe and swung at Morengeone 's face. Morengeone snatched Blinkman's hand out of the air and held it in his own larger hand, squeezing until the other man sank to his knees, screaming in pain.

"Now just be nice, here, Henry. Don't be givin me no trouble after I come out all this way to fix yer contemplation."

Morengeone grabbed Blinkman by the throat and sat him down in a chair in the kitchen.

"You sit there, Henry, goddam it and don't move or I have to fuck you up."

Morengeone walked back into the living room, keeping an eye on Blinkman, who didn't move, and picked up his tool bag. He returned to the kitchen, where Blinkman still sat in the chair, and extracted duct tape from the bag. He duct taped Blinkman to he chair and said, "Now, Henry, that wasn't so bad, was it?"

"Just don't hurt me. I'll do whatever you say," Blinkman said, tears in his eyes.

Morengeone said, "Henry, where be the cups?"

"What?"

"Goddam it Henry, you not listenin again. Where be the cups?"

"The coffee cups?"

"Yeah."

"In that cupboard right behind you."

Morengeone took a cup from the cupboard and poured himself a cup of coffee. He drank it looking at Blinkman.

"Damn if you don't make some ass-kickin coffee, Henry."

"What do you want?" Blinkman sobbed.

"Would you like some coffee, Henry?"

"Yes."

"That's more like it. That my boy. I be fixin you up right away. Fuck me if I don't."

Morengeone put his coffee cup down and extracted three small bottles with colorful labels and a funnel from his bag.

"Here goes, Henry, I get you cleaned out in a jiffy."

Morengeone took a broom and a mop from the corner of the kitchen and taped them to Henry's chair so that the handles went straight up alongside his head. Then, over Blinkman's protests and squirming, he taped Blinkman's head tilted backwards to the two vertical handles. Then he jammed the narrow end of the large funnel into Blinkman's mouth, with Blinkman twisting and struggling, and using the tape, Morengeone fixed the funnel in Blinkman's mouth.

"Now we be ready, Henry," Morengeone said, satisfied that Blinkman was sufficiently taped up.

Blinkman sat in the chair, his arms and legs immobile, his head forced backwards, tilted back, the large funnel in his mouth with tape around the funnel and his mouth so that he could do nothing but make noises in his throat.

"Just to show you I always be thinking of you, Henry, I gonna give you your coffee first, fore I even have a chance to finish mine," Morengeone said, walking over to the coffee maker, still mostly full of hot coffee.

He walked over to the terrified Blinkman, whose eyes were now bulging out of his head, and placing one hand on Blinkman's shoulder, lifted the coffee pot with the other and began to pour the hot coffee down the funnel.

Instantly, Blinkman did his best to yell. Sounds and gurgles came from his throat and through the horn of the funnel. When the hot coffee hit, Blinkman twisted out of Morengeone 's grip and the chair on which he was taped seemed to fly through the air. He landed on the floor on his back with the funnel incongruously still taped to his mouth and coffee running backwards out of the funnel onto the floor.

"Here, motherfucker," Morengeone said. "You ain't finished your coffee." He held the funnel upright and poured in the remainder of the pot, holding it so that Blinkman could not jerk it to the side.

Blinkman struggled, twisted, screamed and gurgled as the hot coffee flowed down the funnel and scalded his throat. He was drowning in scalding coffee.

Some of the coffee escaped out the sides of his mouth where the tape held the funnel in place, but most of it seemed to go down his throat and into his lungs. His eyes bulged in his head and he lay quiet on the floor as the last of the coffee drained from the funnel.

"That's better," Morengeone said. "Not good to be a messy drinker."

Morengeone then turned to the five small bottles he had lined up on the counter top. He broke the seals, got a large mixing bowl from a cupboard, and poured the contents of the bottles into the bowl, mixing them with a large spoon. The first bottle was "Neal's Kick Ass Hot Sauce," the second was "Plug -X Butt Scalder Hot Sauce," and the third was "ASS-PLOSION Hot Sauce"; the fourth was "Day of the Dead Hot Sauce," and the last was "Dr. Anselmo's Colon Reamer Hot Sauce." Bartholomew sniffed the mixture gingerly as he stirred, seemed satisfied that it was properly mixed, and glanced at Brinkman.

Blinkman remained still as Bartholomew stepped over and poured the green, viscous mixture into the funnel still taped to Brinkman's mouth. At first the green fluid backed up at the mouth of the funnel. Then, as it gurgled down the tube of the funnel, small streams of Morengeone 's whup-yo-ass mixture escaped and made crooked channels down the sides of Blinkman's face. Most of the green gel bubbled and globbed and disappeared down the tube of the funnel. It must have been hotter than a blast furnace regulated to full tilt boogey, but Blinkman did not move. His eyes were wide open and his chin was covered with a thin green film.

"Damn, Henry. You doin good. Don't want to get that shit on the floor, though. That don't open you up, nothin will," Morengeone said to the inert form.

He put the empty bottles back in his tool bag, and when the last of the gel had bubbled into Blinkman's mouth, Morengeone cut the funnel loose from the duct tape, packed everything up in the bag, took a last drink of coffee, and studied the body of Blinkman taped to the chair. "Well, I be a motherfucker, Henry," he said. "Smell like you done opened up already. When you good, you good."

CHAPTER THIRTY-THREE

The next day, Tim was hung over. Linda had already gone to work by the time he woke up. Life had bottomed out.

Thank God she was gone. Last night had been a nightmare. She must have shouted at him for hours. It was a wonder the neighbors didn't call the cops. Twice she threw stuff at him. Then she went to the window, opened it, and threw out the ring he had given her. She hated him, pure and simple. And then she got drunk.

Tim drank a pot of coffee and took a shower and finally, he could see through the haze of the night before. Jesus. What was he going to do? No money. No job. No wife. Linda a drunk. And she hated him. Why not? He hated himself.

The whole thing was stupid. Why did he ever think he could get away with it? Insurance companies aren't dumb. The police aren't dumb. His wife wasn't dumb. Why did he ever think she was going to give him millions of dollars? Why would she just hand it over? Because he was so wonderful? Because she couldn't live without him? Yeah, that was the theory. But she did just fine without him once she found out about Linda. What a nutcase he was. He was careless and he deserved what he got. The fuckin bodyguards were probably taking turns screwing her.

So now what? The phone rang. The phone never rang during the day. All Linda's friends knew she was at work. He let it ring until the answering machine picked it up.

The answering machine: "Hello, this is Linda. Your call is so, so, sooo, important to me. Let me call you right back."

Then the caller: "Hello, Tim, this is Linda. I want you out of the house by the time I get home tonight. Leave the key."

That bitch, Tim thought. How am I supposed to do that? I don't have a dime. I can't use my credit card because all my accounts are closed. I don't have a job. All my friends think I'm dead. If I show up somewhere, they might arrest me for pretending I'm dead. Maybe I can claim I had amnesia. But no. They'd ask

Linda. She'd tell them everything. They'd lock me up. My wife won't talk to me, and she's broke anyway. And she's got those two goons over there.

I don't have a lot of choices. I'll kill her when she comes home and then hide the body. I'll take her money and her car and go to Florida. I'll blend into the Spanish community in Miami. They say it's full of criminals and I'd be a criminal, so I could just be one of them. Maybe I could earn a living smuggling drugs. I'd have to get some of that tan in a bottle so I wouldn't look so white. I could wear one of those big hats and dark glasses. I already got the wig and the moustache. I'd be O.K.

What if I didn't kill her and just left now. I could take some of her stuff and sell it for money. Yeah, but if I did that she'd call the cops and they would know I am alive and they'd come looking for me.

What if I got her to let me stay here in the day and then at night I could go to one of those all night porno theatres. Nahhh. I'd get mugged. I'd probably get AIDS.

Maybe I could go back with the bums that pulled me out of the river. I could live with them. Nobody knows who they are or where they came from. But by now they probably know I'm supposed to be dead. They know who I am. They'd turn me in to the cops. They'd ask for a reward. The only reason they helped me before was for the money.

How about my old partner, Jim Duroset? Nahh. He'd go nuts. He'd think I wanted back in. Hell, maybe I do. He'd be afraid of scandal and he'd turn me in faster than any of them. But maybe he'd give me some cash just to go away. I could tell him I don't want to stay at his house, I just want to go away and I need some money. He'd still turn me in. I'm sure he doesn't know Janice turned the money back in to the insurance company. Or maybe he does and he'd be afraid that I want my share of the business back. He'd turn me in just so I'd get arrested and couldn't get the business back.

My parents are dead. Maybe I could go to my Aunt Rita in Portland. Maybe she's dead too. And how am I going to go three thousand miles across the country anyway?

Maybe I could just turn myself into the insurance company and ask them for a few bucks now that my wife gave everything back. They ought to be grateful. Yeah, Tim, they'd turn you in too. They'd say I might not have actually defrauded them, but I tried to, and they'd want me put in jail for that. My wife would end up being a goddam heroine for turning the money back in.

Tim wandered around the apartment, staring out windows, drinking coffee, washing his face, drumming his fingers, turning the TV. on and off, listening to the news without hearing anything, and finally, he found himself dialing the phone. He watched himself doing it. He had no idea why he was dialing the phone, but there it was. He was dialing. He could see it.

"Hello," a subdued voice said.

"Janice, don't hang up. This is Tim. I'm so sorry about the other night and I just need to see you. This is terrible and I didn't mean any of it. Just don't hang up, please."

"Oh, Tim." She began sobbing.

"Don't let those two muscle heads cut you off, please."

"They're outside checking on something."

"Good, can you get away? I need to talk to you now. Right away. Please say you will."

"Tim, why should I? You're with that other woman."

"No I'm not. That's over. It never really started. I need you, not her. Please Janice."

"I want to believe you."

"Then believe me. Just get away from those bozos and meet me."

"Are you telling me the truth? You're not with that woman?"

"No, I'm not with that woman. I need you and I need you now. I'm in trouble. Please, Janice, help me."

"What do you want me to do?"

"I just want you to meet me."

"Where?"

"I don't have a car. Can you meet me at the Coffee Tree shop in Shadyside?"

"Yes, I know where it is. When?"

"As soon as you can get away."

"All right, I'll leave within the hour. It won't be easy getting away, but I will."

"I love you, Janice, and I'll be waiting for you."

Tim paced back and forth on Walnut Street in front of the Coffee Tree Café for an hour. He was wearing his wig and moustache and he felt ridiculous. But he was afraid of running into someone he knew. He looked at the Rolex watches in the jewelry store window. They were the symbol of a normal life. You worked hard and you bought a Rolex watch. And then people knew you had made it. You were a person of respect. You had a life and a place in the world. You were someone. Now, he didn't even exist. He was dead.

Finally, Tim saw Janice emerge from between two buildings. She had parked in the lot behind the stores. She looked right past him as he moved toward her. The gray wig made him look like a derelict.

"Janice, it's me," he said as he approached her.

She stared at him for a moment, and then said, "Oh, my God. Tim. I didn't recognize you. Why do you have that wig on?"

"I'm supposed to be dead, remember?"

"Oh, I forgot," she said.

They got coffee and sat in a corner of the coffee shop. Shoppers came and went. There were not a lot of people. It was a weekday afternoon.

"I don't know why I'm even here," she said.

"You're here because you're my wife and I asked you to come," he said.

"Yes, but you live with that other woman. You just wanted the money. You were going to take the money and leave."

"I was going to do that," he said. "But there's no money now and I'm back. I want you. I'm done with that other woman. We're finished."

"Do you love me?" She asked.

"Yes. I love you. I always have. I just went crazy when I fell off that bridge. I almost died. I don't know what happened to me."

"But you were seeing her before that," Janice said.

"Yes, I was. And I don't know why I did that either. I think I was a little crazy."

"How could you ruin our lives?"

"I didn't mean to, Janice. I swear. There were a lot of pressures at work. The business was always struggling to make more money, get more clients. I was just overwhelmed. I think I cracked."

"Where did you meet this woman?"

"She was a cosmetics salesperson at a department store. I walked through the store one day at lunch time and met her then. I didn't go around looking for women. It just happened."

"Somehow that doesn't make me feel any better."

"Janice, there's nothing I can do. If there was, I'd do it. I love you and I'm hoping you can forgive me."

"Sam and Nick would say you just want the money."

"What money? You gave it back. There is no money. I don't even have a job. If you take me back, we'll have to sell the house. Even if you don't take me back, you'll have to sell the house."

"Why would I take you back?"

"I hope, because you love me."

"You betrayed me."

"I didn't mean to. I'm not perfect. I made a mistake. I didn't want to hurt you. I don't even know why I got involved."

"I can never trust you again."

"Yes you can. You have to. We've been together a long time and we know each other."

"I thought I knew you."

"You do. I want to spend the rest of my life with you. If we ever get straightened out, maybe we can have kids."

"Do you mean it?" Janice said, suddenly animated.

"Yes."

"Oh, Tim. That would be wonderful."

"I have to tell you something. This was meant to happen. When I was in that river in the car and I thought I was going to die and I couldn't get out, you know what saved me?"

"No. It sounds awful."

"You remember that knife you gave me?"

"Yes."

"Well, I got it out of my pocket and hit the window with the point and it shattered. Otherwise I would be dead now."

"Couldn't you just hit the glass and break it?" she asked.

"No. When you're underwater, the pressure is the same on both sides of the glass and it won't break unless you hit it a sharp blow with something hard. That knife was the only thing I had that would break it. And if you hadn't given me that knife, I wouldn't be here."

She reached over and took his hand. "I guess it was meant to be, then," she said, smiling.

"I want to come back, Janice."

He leaned over and kissed her. She pulled off the moustache and he kissed her again.

"Oh Tim, I love you."

"I love you too."

"So you're coming back to me?"

"If you'll have me."

"Only if you never do this again."

"I promise," he said. "Never again."

She stared at him for a time, and then said, "I have a nice surprise for you. You don't have to worry about how we'll get along. I didn't give the money back. I just told you that."

Tim was dumbfounded. He just looked at her with his mouth open. "You mean you still have it?"

"Yes."

"Three million?"

"Well, no."

"Oh, it's those bodyguards isn't it? They took some. How much did they take?"

"I haven't paid them anything yet."

"How much are you going to pay them?"

"A million dollars."

"What?" He said in an outraged voice.

"Tim, they saved my life."

Warning lights went off in Tim's head and he backed off. He didn't want to seem too interested in the money after he'd just skated around disaster. But he couldn't help it. He began thinking about Linda. Maybe they could make it after all. He could call her up and tell her that the money wasn't gone. They could still have a life. They could run away. She could have all the new clothes she wanted.

All he'd have to do is get Janice to give him a million. But no, she'd never do that now. She'd suspect. She'd know. Asking her for the million dollars would fuck everything up.

What was wrong with him? He'd just escaped poverty, arrest, conviction, imprisonment, dishonor, infamy and ruin, and as soon as he'd escaped, he was trying to jump back into it. Take what the Lord is giving you and shut up about it, he thought, angry with himself.

"You're right. They deserve it for saving your life. And besides, that still leaves us two million."

"Well, no, not really," she said.

"You spent it on something else?" He said.

"I didn't spend anything."

"Then why don't you have two million left?"

"Because Sam negotiated with the construction company that fixed that bridge and he agreed to pay me three million dollars if I would withdraw the lawsuit."

Tim's eyes nearly popped out of his head. "He's going to pay you three million dollars?"

"No."

"But you just said. . ."

"He already paid it."

"He already paid it. You mean you have six million dollars?"

"Yes."

There was a pause while Tim took this all in.

"Six million dollars," he muttered, "And this bodyguard got this for you?"

"Yes. You should be nice to him."

"I take back all those bad things I said about him."

Tim's mind began racing again. He had just gone from dead meat on the chopping block to the luckiest man in the world. His impulse was to get away with the money before somebody took it away from them. He was suddenly apprehensive.

"Why did this contractor pay you three million dollars?" He asked.

"Because he killed you," Janice said.

"And the insurance company paid you three million dollars also because I am dead," he said.

"Yes."

"So if anyone finds out I am not dead, all this money goes back," he said.

"I guess," she said.

"Then we need to keep this a secret, Honey. Our lives together depend on this being a secret."

"Well, the only people who know are Sam and Nick, and they're not going to tell anyone," she said.

"And Linda," Tim said.

CHAPTER THIRTY-FOUR

Tim walked back to Linda's apartment, a jangle of nerves. He was wired on the coffee and even more wired on the six million dollars. Three hours ago he had been a stumble bum and now he was a fucking millionaire. She was going to take him back. He was going to be rich. He was going to be safe. He was going to live in some castle on the coast of France. He was going to be there with Janice and not Linda, but that was a minor glitch. Jesus. Six million dollars. All he had to do now was keep his cool. He'd have to plan, just like he did when he clawed his way out of the river. He'd figure it out. This could go wrong yet. He couldn't let that happen.

Linda was the problem. If she blabbed, he'd be fucked and six million dollars poorer. When you put it that way, he didn't have many options. He wasn't a killer, but in this situation...

Tim spent the rest of the afternoon gathering his stuff into a large duffle bag and cleaning the apartment. He knew that his fingerprints were everywhere and he had read that they could trace DNA from hair, so he wore a stocking cap and surgical gloves and wiped everything down, even the dishes, and vacuumed everything twice. He put a new bag in the vacuum and when he was through, he put both vacuum bags in the trash chute in the hallway. Then he did the laundry, stripping the sheets from the bed and taking down the towels in the bathroom.

Linda was due home in an hour. He took his duffle bag down to the basement storage room where Linda had a locker. No one ever went in there. It was dark and a little cold in the locker room, but Tim sat there on his duffle bag, leaning back against the wire fencing of the locker and thought about what he needed to do.

Maybe this wasn't wise. Maybe there was another way. He was about to do something he couldn't undo. Once it was done, it was done forever. Once he killed her, she would always be dead. He would always be a killer. He couldn't bring her back.

Then he thought, if you took a survey of every person in the world and you told them, you can keep six million dollars if you kill a woman, how many would do it? Most of them, he concluded. Nearly every damned one.

Nonetheless, he was afraid. But why? Probably his Catholic childhood. Priests and nuns always harping on what you had to do or not do. And always ending with the requirement that you give your money to the church. When it's all said and done, they are just like me, he thought. Me and the church. We're like all the other criminals in the world. All of us are just out for what we can get, but only the Church has a whole organized set-up to get them what they want.

Let's be honest, he thought, People like to be high and mighty. They'd say they would never do what I'm gonna do. But they're liars. They would do it. People cheat each other all the time. What I'm doing is just cheating on a big scale, but it's all the same in principle. I been cheating people in my business for years. And Janice, she'll be all upset about this, but she's been living off my cheating our whole marriage and she never got bothered about that. It's all bullshit. You take what you can get. That's the bottom line.

Tim fell into a fitful sleep, mumbling to himself, his body occasionally jerking as he slept. He dreamed of standing on the bank of a pond and watching a duckling swim toward him. Suddenly, something came from beneath the water and grabbed the duckling, dragging it under. Tim didn't know what to do. It was as if he himself were being dragged under. He dived into the water to save the duckling but it was dark and he could see almost nothing. Occasionally weeds would brush past his face and unknown objects would glance off his body. Then he could see bubbles, and it was as if he were now in the sinking car. There was an air pocket up there. He had to get to it. He swam desperately for the air pocket. He kept swimming. His lungs were exploding. He knew it was there... and then he jerked awake, lurching into a sitting position, covered with sweat, gasping for air.

Tim sat in the basement locker for another twenty minutes, recovering from the nightmare and waiting for Linda to come home. By five thirty, there was movement upstairs in the apartments on the first floor. Linda would be getting home about now.

She would get home, open the door, see that the place was all cleaned up and he wasn't there, and she would take her bath. That's what she always did when she got home. She would be in the bathtub for half an hour and then she would start thinking about dinner.

At five forty-five, Tim left the basement and walked up to Linda's apartment on the second floor. The newspaper he had left propped up against the door was gone. She was home. He quietly slipped his key in the lock and opened the door. He could hear water running in the bathtub. He closed the apartment door quietly and tiptoed to the bathroom. The door was partly open and he could see that Linda just stepped into the tub and was beginning to lower herself into the water. When she was in the water, he opened the door. She jumped and made a little sound.

"Oh my God, Tim, you scared me to death."

"Hello," he said.

"What are you doing here? I told you to leave."

"I just wanted to see you before I left," he said.

"I want you out of here."

"I'll be out of here in a minute," he said, picking up the radio he had moved into the bathroom from the kitchen and plugging it in."

"What are you doing? Get out of here."

Tim lobbed the radio into the bathtub with an underhanded pitch. Linda screamed when she saw what he was doing, but she couldn't extract herself from the tub before the radio got there.

It never got there. It sailed through the air until it was caught up short by the cord, which stopped it in mid air and brought it crashing down on the bathroom floor. The cord was too short.

"Sonofabitch," Tim yelled, angry, scared, and frustrated. Now what? This was supposed to be a hands-off, clean killing. She would fry in the water and he would unplug the radio when she was dead. Now what? She knows. She's going to resist.

Linda was lifting herself out of the water and screaming "You want to kill me. Help. Help. He's trying to kill me."

Tim grabbed her arm and tried to push her back down, but the arm was slippery with water and he fell into her, his head near her stomach, as she half- stood in the bathtub. She grabbed his hair, screaming, and he lifted her legs out from under her, splashing her back into the water. But she had a death grip on his hair and he was pulled into the water himself as she went down. She was amazingly strong and was pushing his face into the water. He placed his hands on the bottom of the tub and pushed up to get his head above water, dripping with bubble bath and gasping for air.

She was screaming when he came up. With one hand, she pounded on his face. With the other she tore at his hair and tried to push him down again into the water. He was too strong and he tore his head away from her grip, but he didn't know what to do next. He grabbed a wash cloth that was on the side of the tub and, holding the hand that was hitting him, he jammed the washcloth in Linda's face with the other hand. It took her by surprise and she went backwards, and then under the water. He now held her face down with both hands, letting the washcloth go. His fingers were directly on her face, and then they weren't. She damned near bit off the middle finger in his right hand and he jerked the hand out of the water, screaming in pain.

Linda's head came up like a sea creature, spewing water, covered with matted hair, gasping for air, and attacking all at the same time. Tim was still on his knees next to the bathtub, and her body seemed to follow the head in an upward arc that ended with her teeth sunk into Tim's right shoulder. Tim screamed louder. She had bitten into a nerve that made his whole left arm go numb. Instantly, in terrific pain, he bellowed and swung a hook at her left ear. The blow connected and she froze, stunned. She seemed to wilt into a semi-consciousness half in and half out of the tub. Tim got to his feet, holding his bleeding shoulder and grabbed the radio.

Breathing hard, he stood back, looked at the woman draped over the edge of the tub, and swung the radio on its cord. He hit her head with the flying radio and then swung it in a bigger arc, banging it off the ceiling, and into her head again. He hit her a dozen times, watching the water and the blood splatter on the walls and ceiling as the radio made its lethal arc. Suddenly, Tim felt nauseous. He was in the room but not in the room. He stood outside of himself listening to the radio thunk into Linda's head. Finally, she no longer moved and blood covered the floor next to the tub.

Tim stood against the door of the bathroom, feeling sick, his knees weak, injured, his shoulder covered with blood, patches of his hair pulled out, his shirt wet down to his pants with water, bubble bath and blood. Suddenly, he needed to throw up, and his feet moved him to the toilet. He slipped in the blood as he moved and he fell, bumping his head on the edge of the toilet. His head throbbing, his ears ringing, his vision blurred, he barely had the wherewithal to vomit into the bowl. The yellow-orange stream of vomit with lumps in it shot out of his mouth and stained the bowl. He flushed the toilet and washed most of it away.

Collecting his wits, what was left of them, he leaned against the door and struggled to figure out what he had to do. He had to get the body back in the tub, clean out any of his hair that he could find, clean up the blood and the vomit, and get the hell out of there. He got the body back in the tub and turned on the shower to wash down any traces of hair or skin that she might have on her. He even scraped her nails. Then he poured drain cleaner down the drain to destroy any evidence that might be in the trap.

Tim struggled with the wig and the mustache, then he limped down to the basement for his duffle bag and left the building, wet, injured, shaken, sick and scared out of his mind.

CHAPTER THIRTY-FIVE

"You must have the wrong number, Mr. Bartholomew," the butler said.

"I ain't got no wrong number. And it's Mr. Morengeone, not Mr. Bartholomew. I callin Mr. Badersault and this be his number. Now put him on."

"I thought you said your name was Mr. Bartholomew."

"No, cracker, I said my name was Bartholomew Morengeone."

"Isn't that what I just said?"

"No honkey motherfucker, it ain't be. I Bartholomew Morengeone, not Morengeone Baltholomew."

"My apologies, Sir. But I'm afraid you have the wrong number."

"Let me try again. I be Mr. Morengeone. Not Mr. Bartholomew. Got that? Tell the boss who it be."

"I've heard of Morengeone Grapefruit Drink," the butler said. "Are you calling about that?"

"Now I'm gettin' upset. I ain't callin about no grapefruit, Ratfuck."

"I'm sorry Sir, but there is no one here by the name of Ratfuck."

"Oh, My God. What I gotta go thru here. You too dumb for me. Put the house nigger on. He know what to do."

"I'm sorry Sir, but there is no house nigger. If you're calling the Ratfucks, they may have a house nigger, but we don't. Haven't for some years."

"Now you hidin the house nigger. Goddam it. Put the sonofabitch on."

"If I may be so bold sir, directory assistance may be able to locate the Ratfuck residence. And if they do, then your can speak with their house nigger."

"Just let me talk to the count, you moron."

"Who should I say is calling, Sir?"

"Now we getting somewhere. Tell him Morengeone is callin."

"What is this about, Mr. Bartholomew?"

"Just put him on you dumb cracker. Don't ask me no questions and don't sell me short, or I fuck you up."

"If you're trying to sell something, Mr. Badersault doesn't take commercial calls."

"Don't make me come over there, motherfucker. I come over there, you gonna wish you wuz trampled by wild horses."

"Very good, Sir. Let me connect you to the stables."

"No dumb shit, not the stables. I want the head man...."

The phone rang and a woman answered.

"Stables, Maybella here."

"Maybella, this be Bartholomew Morengeone ."

"Bartholomew what?"

"Morengeone."

"Is this some kind of joke?"

"This ain't no joke Maybella."

"Do you know me?"

"No, Maybella... but I..." Morengeone said.

"You some kinda pervert?"

"I ain't sure what you mean, Maybell."

"Maybella."

"Look here, Maybella. I just be the nigger works for Mr. Badersault."

"I don't go out with no niggers. So just shut yourself up."

"No Maybella, I don't wanna go out wit you. I..."

"What's wrong with me? Not good enough for you?"

"Oh, fuck. No Maybella, you're jest fine. I onliest tryin to get to the boss."

"Oh. That's it, you piece of shit. You like me but you want to go out with him. Goddam fairy. Well I got news for you, he won't go out with you either. I'm Miss Affirmative Action next to him."

"No, he know me."

"He no you?"

"No, he know me. You know, know."

"If the boss already said no to you, what you think I'm gonna say? I think you're high on something."

"No Maybella. I ain't high. I workin for the boss."

"Now I know you're full of shit. The boss don't have no truck with niggers. I'm gonna connect you to the shithouse."

"No, no, Maybella... "

There was clicking sound, then a buzz, then ringing.

"Shithouse."

* * *

Three hours later, a lopsided 1963 Cadillac convertible lunged into the Badersault estate. It belched blue smoke as it ticked along the tree-lined asphalt driveway, rounding the easy curves for the mile drive from the road to the big house. The valve lifters made so much noise that the motor sounded like an industrial sized sewing machine. A belligerent looking black man sat behind the wheel, his bandaged wrist hanging straight down alongside the car as it crept along past the carefully trimmed, watered and mowed grounds.

As the car pulled up in front of the estate's main entrance, three large men in T shirts converged, two on the driver's side, one on the passenger side. Simultaneously, the men on both sides of the car opened the doors. The driver's side men grabbed Morengeone and unceremoniously pulled him out of the car. As soon as the men grabbed his arm, Morengeone bellowed in pain and yelled for them to watch his injury.

Meanwhile, the car ticked along, creeping up the driveway, headed for a flower bed. The passenger side man dove into the front seat and jammed the transmission into park with a growling clunk that stopped the car short. The two men who had dragged Morengeone out of the car were maneuvering him to the edge of the driveway.

"Easy, cracker," Morengeone yelled. "Easy."

One of the men tripped Morengeone and put him face-down on the driveway where both men patted him down.

"He's clean," one said.

"Sure, I clean." Morengeone said. "I want to see the count."

"Who should we say is calling?" One of the muscle men grinned.

"Bartholomew Morengeone ."

"Bartholomew what?"

"Let him go," Badersault said from the front door. "He works for me. Let him go."

Morengeone shrugged off the grip of his captor and walked to the front door, where Badersault stood. The folds in Morengeone's face glistened and shined and bristled with stubble.

"What are you doing here?" Badersault said. "You are supposed to be watching that house."

"That what I come to talk to you about," Morengeone said. "I tried to call, but that cracker butler of yours wouldn't let me talk to you."

"Why not?"

"The motherfucker..."

"Never mind. Come in here."

Badersault led Morengeone into the library and had him sit in one of the chairs next to the fireplace, which was now covered, in the warm months, with a huge bronze fan. The house itself was cool, both from its stone structure and twenty foot ceilings and also from central air conditioning.

The afternoon light warmed the leather bound books, the gold lettering on their spines gleaming here and there where the light hit them just right. The windows lining the outside wall were ablaze with sun.

Badersault motioned for Morengeone to sit and said, "What do you have to report?"

Morengeone sat in one of the leather armchairs facing the fireplace. "I seen the dead man. The man they show in the papers. The one 'sposed to be killed on the bridge. He just walked in. Big as fuckin life. He alive."

"You mean Timothy Brannigan?" Badersault said, his eyes wide and intense.

"Yeah. The bitch's husband. The one live in that house I been watchin. I been watchin for one white motherfucker and I grab aholt of another."

"Are you sure?"

"Hell yes, I sure. I seen his picture in the paper after he drowned hisself."

Morengeone reached in his pocket and pulled out a folded photographic print of Tim Brannigan getting out of a cab in front of his house. Morengeone had an eight power binocular with a digital camera built in. It was a piece of junk, but it would produce pixilated 8 x 10's shot at eight power. Morengeone had stopped at a drug store and had the print made on the way to Badersault's mansion.

"I'll be a sonofabitch," Badersault fumed. "I been scammed." His large head got bright red and his body began to shake. "Get your men together and kill 'em all. Kill the woman, the husband and those two men with them. Nobdody scams Count von Badersault. Nobody. Hear me? Nobody."

"Now we talkin," Morengeone said. "Can I kill the dog too?"

CHAPTER THIRTY-SIX

The day Janice met Tim in Shadyside, she arrived back home about four o'clock. She parked her car in the garage next to the Landcruiser used by Sam and Nick and encountered an irate Sam.

"What's wrong with you?" He said. "What is it about danger that you don't understand?"

"I had to meet Tim," she said, pushing past him and into the house.

Sam followed her up the stairs and into the kitchen, where she got a glass, ice, and Scotch from a cabinet. She poured herself a Scotch and water and turned.

"Anyone else want a drink?"

"No thanks," Sam said. "What was so important that you had to leave Nick and me behind?"

"Sam," she said, turning to face him, her drink a shield between them. "I appreciate everything you've done, and if you'll check the account number you gave me, I deposited a million dollars in that account on my way home. You're free now and I thank you. I no longer need you."

"Don't say that," Nick said from the background, watching the exchange between Sam and Janice. "Every time somebody says that, things start to go wrong."

"He's right," Sam said. "We know about the payment. Our bank emailed us. And we thank you. It was very generous, but if you'll permit it, we would just like to make sure you're all right before we leave."

"I'm all right. Look at me," Janice smiled. "Tim and I are going away. We'll be fine."

"That's your business and we will not interfere," Sam said. "I assume you have considered everything Cochran had to tell you and you have made up your mind after considering whatever Cochran had to say."

"Yes."

"I took the liberty of calling Cochran and telling him that you were gone and that I anticipated you would be going away with your husband," Sam said.

"And what did he say?" Janice said.

"He said that if you are going to be with your husband, here or anywhere else, you need to move your money out of the country, because if anyone recognizes Tim, all your money in the country could get tied up."

"How could anyone recognize Tim?" She said.

"Suppose he was in an auto accident. Or he dropped dead on the sidewalk. His fingerprints might be taken and he might be identified," Sam said.

"But how would that lead them to know it's Tim?" She said.

"He has a gun permit. They take your finger prints," Nick said. "That puts your prints in an international data base. They would match his prints to the data base and they would find out."

"We'll have fake passports," Janice said.

"Suppose the supplier of your fake passports gets busted and plea bargains by giving up the names of everyone he's made passports for," Sam said. "They identify you and freeze your accounts."

"So what do we do?" She said.

"Cochran tells me he has general power of attorney for you. Call him and authorize him to transfer all your funds to the Swiss and Caymon Island accounts he already set up," Sam said. "The money will be accessible to you, but it can't be frozen if they find out Tim is alive, and if you follow Cochran's advice about where you can and cannot go, they won't be able to extradite you."

Janice made the call and Cochran set in motion the machinery to transfer roughly five million dollars to Swiss and Caymon numbered accounts. He had regular dealings with Mellon Bank, where most of Janice's money was sitting, and he faxed them his power of attorney. The accounts in Mellon and in all the other U.S. banks would be transferred by mid-morning the next day.

"We wish you the best," Sam said. "I can't say that I'm glad about you going off with your husband, but that is for you, not for me to decide. I hope it works out well."

"I'm sure it will, and I appreciate your concern," she said. "You and Nick saved my life and helped me in so many ways that I can never thank you. But I want you to know that I understand what you have done and I am grateful."

"Our pleasure," Nick said. "When is Tim coming?"

"He said he'll be here tomorrow. He has some things he has to take care of first," Janice said.

"All right," Sam said. "We'll stay one more night."

Nick made pasta and salad for dinner. Ronin had crunchy dog food.

Sam and Nick took turns on the monitors and Ronin patrolled the inside perimeter, just as on any other night. Janice went to bed around ten. Sam and Nick had the eleven o'clock news on while they heated some water for tea when the story broke. Linda Girard, employed as a secretary at the law firm of Dingle and Killem, was found brutally murdered in her apartment earlier this evening. Homicide detectives had no suspects at this time. Her picture flashed full frame on the screen.

Sam and Nick looked at each other and went into immediate action. Sam went into Janice's bedroom to wake her up and Nick began dismantling the TV. monitors.

"What's wrong?" Janice sleepily said.

"Tim has killed his lady friend. It's only a matter of time before he is caught, if he isn't caught already, and once he's caught, the police will be coming here," Sam said.

She was wide awake now. "What do we do?" She said.

"Pack whatever you can pack in ten minutes. We'll be leaving as soon as the truck is packed," Sam said. "I've got to help Nick."

Nick and Sam got all of the monitors into the back of the truck within a few minutes. They were connected to the cameras by radio signal, so there were no wires. Spare rifles, explosives and ammunition that had been stashed at strategic locations was gathered up and packed in the truck. Within twenty minutes, Sam, Nick, Janice and Ronin were in the Landcruiser driving away from the house.

By now Janice was more awake and more skeptical. "How do you know it's her?"

"Her picture was on TV.," Nick said.

"How do you know Tim did it?"

"Just a coincidence, huh?" Sam said.

"Why do you think he'll be caught? I need to be there when he gets home tomorrow," she said.

"He'll get caught because he doesn't know what he's doing," Nick said. "We'll be there tomorrow to pick him up if he hasn't been caught by then, but you'll be in a safe location."

"I'm sorry," she said, sheepishly. "You guys really are looking out for me. It's just that I love my husband. I'm afraid for him."

"We'll bring him back for you if we can," Sam said. "Don't worry about that. But it doesn't do you any good to get arrested if he brings the police to the house."

"Where are you taking me?"

"We're going to a safe house," Sam said.

Forty minutes later they were in the Bloomfield section of Pittsburgh. The Bloomfield safe house was a row house on an isolated street with a three car garage connected to the house by a tunnel. Sam pulled the truck in and helped Nick unload the armaments. Janice made coffee and Ronin was glad to be home. He plopped down on the dog bed in the kitchen and didn't move.

By the time Sam called Cochran, it was one-thirty. He explained the situation. Cochran had only one thing to say.

"Get her out of Pittsburgh."

CHAPTER THIRTY-SEVEN

The next morning about eleven a.m., the day after Tim left Linda's lifeless body in the bathroom of her apartment, he arrived by cab at his former residence. In the cab, he removed the wig and mustache. There were no neighbors in his neighborhood close enough to see who came and went from his house. In any event, neither he nor Janice knew anyone who lived in the development.

He would be safe without the wig and he was tired of wearing it. The cabby could think whatever he wanted. By the time the police figured anything out, he and Janice would be long gone. He paid for the cab with money he had taken from Linda's wallet.

Morengeone, three hundred yards away behind a bushy fencerow in a field that overlooked the housing development had seen Sam drive into the garage early in the morning. Now he had Tim in his eight power lens.

"Time to go, motherfuckers," he said to Whipdick and Jo Bob, who were leaning on the car trading obscenities.

As Morengeone watched, Tim approached the house. He knocked with trepidation, hoping that nothing had gone wrong, that the muscle heads had not made off with the money and his wife or talked her out of going away with him. He was just beginning to fantasize about what he would do to Janice when the door opened and Sam told him to step in. Sam put him against the wall and patted him down and then told him to go into the living room and sit down.

"Coffee?" Sam said.

"Where's my wife?" Tim asked.

"Coffee?"

"No. Where's my wife?" Tim was beginning to panic. It had actually happened. They had taken Janice and the money and now they were going to kill him.

"I'm having coffee," Sam said. "Your wife's in a safe place."

Sam carried his steaming mug into the living room and saw Tim staring at the .45 on his belt. They're actually going to kill me right now, Tim thought. He's going to do it. He wanted to kill me from the first.

Sam saw the look of fear and panic on Brannigan's face.

"Take it easy, Mr. Brannigan. We heard the news report. We know you killed the girl. We knew that you might be caught. If you were, the police would come here and maybe arrest your wife as an accomplice, and in any case, they would freeze all her assets. So we moved her to a safe place."

"How do I know this is true?" Brannigan said.

Sam pulled out a strange looking cell phone. "She'll be waiting for your call. The CIA can trace any call anywhere, but if you keep this to about thirty seconds, it will take them a long time to trace it. Got it?"

"Yeah."

Sam dialed the phone and handed it to Tim.

After a long interval, the connection was made and Nick answered.

"I want to talk to Janice," Tim said.

"Wait," Nick said.

"Tim, oh Tim! It's you," Janice said.

"Are you all right?" he said.

"Yes. Sam and Nick moved me to a new location. Are you all right?"

"Yes. Where are you?"

"I can't tell you that," Janice said. "Sam is going to bring you here. Oh, Tim. Did you kill that girl?"

Silence.

"Tim, talk to me. Did you do it? I have to know."

"I did it for us, Janice. There was no other way. She knew I was alive. We would have lost all the money."

"I'm so scared, Tim. I can't believe you killed her."

"I didn't have a choice, Honey."

"Come to me as soon as you can," she said. "I need you to hold me."

And then the phone went dead. Sam opened his mouth and was beginning to say something about getting ready to go when the front picture window exploded. He heard the staccato full auto fire of a submachine gun.

Sam did not even realize he had moved until he looked down and saw a wide-eyed Tim underneath him. They were both on the floor in the living room. The submachine gun chatter was to Sam's right, down by the garage, a shotgun was continuing to blast the hell out of the curtains on the front window, leaving holes in the plaster where the double ought buck pellets hit, shattering wood, knickknacks, and shredding any sort of window covering. Simultaneously, Sam heard shooting in the back of the house. Glass from the large sliding glass doors shattered and sprayed all over the kitchen floor. The large kitchen window also exploded.

Okay. There were three shooters, two shotguns, one subgun. Subgun in front, shotgun in back, shotgun two at the garage. Grabbing Tim by a trembling wrist, Sam said, "Follow me. We're crawling on our bellies. Don't get too far behind. Don't think about what you're doing. Just do it. We're going to the garage."

Double ought buck rounds shredded the sheer curtains on the narrow window next to the heavy front door as they crawled beneath it. Shards of glass covered both Sam and Tim and Sam glanced back to make sure Tim was still coming. He was. More rounds hit the window, blowing it out completely, and then they hit the door.

When Sam got to the inner garage door, he stood and pulled Tim to his feet, drew his .45, and peeked out the door leading from the house to the garage. The overhead door was full of holes and shafts of light shone through, illuminating the dust that been kicked up by the bullets hitting the car, ticking into the cinderblock walls and splattering the shelves in the garage. There was a pause in the sub-gun fire and Sam grabbed Tim's hand, slapped the Audi keys into his palm and shouted, "Go to the airport."

"What about you?"

"I'll be fine. I need to stay here to take care of these guys. You just get outa here. Drive right through 'em. The car is bulletproof."

Tim looked apprehensively into the garage, and when he looked back, Sam was gone. He had gone back toward the front door and the kitchen. He would draw them into the house. He knew the layout. They didn't. An advantage for him. Then he heard the garage door.

"Damn." He had meant for him to drive through it, not open it up. All he had to do was drive. The car would protect him.

Instantly, there was the staccato burst of sub-gun fire. Only it was louder this time. Almost as if the guy was in the garage. Sam crawled back toward the garage door. Now he heard shouting and scuffling. Tim's voice. Not good. They had Tim. The shooter had dived under the garage door as soon as it began to open, fired a burst of full auto into the driver's side windows, scared the hell out of Tim, yanked him out the driver's side door, and thrown him on the floor. Sam knew what had happened as soon as he heard the scuffling.

Sam peeked out the garage door, listening at the same time for someone coming from the front door area behind him. What he saw in the garage was disheartening. The gunman had Tim on the far side of the car and was holding a MAC 10 to his head.

Sam took another quick peek and got a glimpse of a second gunman coming into the garage, now that the door was wide open. Both were on the other side of the car. The new gunman had a shotgun. As if to emphasize the point, a pattern of double ought buck appeared in the door next to Sam, splintering it and sending shards of wood flying. Sam couldn't shoot because of Tim.

A voice came out of the hall behind him from inside the house. The voice was around a corner, near the kitchen, past the front door.

"Here's the thing, white boy, you fucked."

Sam shot three rounds into the wall toward where he imagined the voice was coming from.

"These houses ain't much, white boy, but that little gun a yers ain't gonna go through three walls to get to me. And my boy out the garage gonna blow the brains out that little bitch you been protectin, less, that is, you throw down the gun. You got five seconds to throw that gun out the garage or we start comin at you from both directions and we kill the bitch before we start."

"Okay. Okay," Sam said. "Tell them not to shoot when I toss the gun out."

"You hear that, Whipdick. Don't shoot so's he can toss the gun."

"Okay," Whipdick said.

"Here comes the gun," Sam said.

The sound of steel skidding across concrete was loud enough that Morengeone could hear it from his place of concealment near the kitchen. It was a clicking, metallic sound.

"All right, boy, now crawl out the garage on all fours," Morengeone said.

Sam slowly opened the door fully and started crawling out toward the parked Audi.

"Stop," Whipdick yelled. "He's in the garage."

Morengeone clambered down the short hall and around the corner to where the open garage door was visible. He could see Sam's boot where he had stopped crawling. He moved up to the door and held his shotgun on Sam's back. Whipdick moved Tim around from the other side and threw him down on the floor next to Sam, who was still on all fours. Tim's pants were stained from where his bladder had failed him.

Morengeone kicked Sam's legs out from under him and Sam was spread-eagled on the cement floor. Morengeone put the barrel of the shotgun to the back of his neck and patted him down for other weapons. Joe Bob moved around to the garage door side of the garage and trained his shotgun on Sam. Whipdick trained his sub-gun on them from the rear of the garage.

"Roll over, bitch," Morengeone said. "I guess you not be goin to no airport now."

Sam rolled over. Morengeone patted him down from the front.

"He's clean," Morengeone said.

"Joe Bob, come with me down to the Cadillac. We get the duct tape, the ropes, the plastic bags and all that shit, and get rid of these shotguns. They too obvious. Whipdick, move over here so the sun's not in you eyes and cover these motherfuckers till we get back."

Morengeone and Joe Bob lowered their shotguns and walked out of the garage, toward the Cadillac, parked on he street in front of the house. Morengeone bent down and picked up Sam's .45 on the way down the driveway.

Sam faced the open garage door, lying on his back, his arms behind his head, Tim next to him lying on his stomach.

"Whipdick," Sam said, "That what they call you?"

"Yes, White Devil," Whipdick said.

"Can you whip a man with your dick?" Sam teased.

"Yes, White Devil, and not only that, but I can cut a man in two with this gun. I pull the trigger and I sweep across his body. And then I have two white devils instead of one."

"Well, as a last request," Sam said, "Since you're gonna kill us, I sure would be honored if I could see your dick. It'd be my last thought on earth, admiring a dick like that."

"We can do that, white devil," Whipdick said, stepping toward Sam so that his feet straddled Sam's upturned toes. "I need to take a piss anyway, and you can see my dick while I piss all over you. I'd piss on the girl too, but he already pissed on himself."

Whipdick walked up next to Sam, still lying on his back with his hands locked behind his head, shifted the MAC 10 to his left hand and began to unzip his pants with his right. Sam lowered his right hand beneath his collar and gripped the tip of a weapon that Morengeone had missed. It was taped to the center of Sam's back and the tip was just below his shirt collar. It was a Cold Steel throwing device that consisted of a hefty piece of solid steel rod, a little bigger around at its midpoint than a quarter, tapering down to sharp points at each end, about fifteen inches long and weighing close to two pounds. In the second when Whipdick's fingers had not yet found purchase on the MAC 10, Sam extracted the steel rod and threw it with all his strength at Whipdick's center of mass. He was three feet away. The pointed steel rod struck him in the solar plexus and penetrated his entire torso, sticking out his back. He sunk to his knees with a "Whuuuf."

Sam scrambled to his feet, grabbed Whipdick's weapon, and handed Tim his spare set of keys to the Audi.

"Go to the airport, short term parking. Nick will be there with Janice within a few hours. Don't worry about them shooting at you when you drive out. Go."

As Tim struggled to get into the car, Sam went to the opening of the garage and looked for Morengeone and Joe Bob. They were fifty yards away in front of the house. As soon as Sam had the weapon leveled, he let off a short burst from the Mac 10. Bullets clanked and thunked all over the white Cadillac and both Morengeone and Joe Bob hit the dirt. The Mac 10 was an unfamiliar weapon, and hitting at fifty yards was not going to happen. Tim finally got the car started and the tires squealed as the big Audi shot backwards out of the garage and onto the driveway. As the Audi approached the curb, both Joe Bob and Morengeone, now crouching behind the white Cadillac, fired at the car, but to no effect. Tim jammed the gear selector into drive and the Audi launched down the street.

"Motherfucker," Morengeone said.

Realizing that both he and Joe Bob were armed with weapons that weren't too effective beyond fifteen yards, he pushed Joe Bob towards the rear door of the Cadillac on the protected side of the car.

"Get in," Morengeone hissed at Joe Bob. They both got into the Cadillac, Morengeone in the driver's seat and Joe Bob in the back. The Cadillac roared and blew out black smoke on starting. Morengeone jammed the selector into reverse and the car, backing up, lunged into the driveway toward the house. A burst from the Mac 10 shattered the rear window and both tail lights and put holes in the trunk. Inside the car, Morengeone and Jo Bob were both sprayed with pellets of glass, which flew all over the inside and bounced off the windscreen and the dashboard as the rounds from the Mac 10 blew out the rear window. When bullets hit the trunk, it sounded like the car was being pelted with stones. Morengeone wheeled the Cadillac around so that it was angled in the driveway and the left side of the car was shielded from Sam's fire. Both he and Joe Bob baled out as soon as the car stopped, and none too soon, because a new twenty round burst from the Mac 10 hit the side of the car, shattering the passenger windows front and rear and punching a ragged line of holes in both doors. At least now they were close enough to use the shotguns.

Joe Bob came up over the trunk and Morengeone came up over the hood and fired their shotguns into the garage. It was an impressive barrage of ten rounds, five from each gun, and Sam headed for the deeper cover of the interior door leading into the house. Shotgun pellets thwacked, thunked, pinged and even ricocheted around the inside of the garage. Sam's main objective, getting Tim out of there, was accomplished, and now all he had to concentrate on was not getting killed. He had exhausted the four magazines for the Mac 10 he'd found on Whipdick's body and was amazed that Morengeone and his pal stayed around after taking that kind of fire. They were in close now and he was left only with his Glock Model 27 in the ankle holster that Morengeo had not found.

Retreating into the house, he would have a slight edge not only in knowing the terrain, but also in using the more maneuverable pistol around corners and in tight places. Shotguns were intimidating, but they were awkward in houses unless you had a straight shot down a hall.

Sam positioned himself flat against the wall inches from the door leading to the garage. He could hear the two men in the garage moving toward the door where he stood. There was some muffled talking in the garage and then he heard Morengeone say, "You go first." Right after that, the barrel of a shotgun poked through the door, as if it were a live thing probing for his location.

Sam grabbed the shotgun barrel with his left hand and yanked Joe Bob partially into the doorway. Sam himself was now exposed in the doorway, but

Joe Bob's gun was tied up and Morengeone could not shoot because Joe Bob was between him and Sam. That wasn't a problem for Sam. He fired twice, sending two 180 grain hollowpoints into Joe Bob's throat, instantly severing his carotid artery and destroying his voice box, killing him within seconds and disabling him instantly. Immediately, Sam felt Joe Bob release his grip on the gun. The shot that severed the carotid artery exited the neck and hit Morengeone in the cheek, spraying him with Joe Bob's blood, the ragged hollow point lodging in Morengeone 's face like a bloody star-shaped piece of jewelry.

Instantly, Morengeone knew that he had been hit and he instinctively ducked and retreated. What he didn't know was how badly he had been hit. There was blood all over his hands and face and Joe Bob was on the floor with blood spurting out his neck. This was no time to fuck around. Morengeone retreated so fast that Sam could not even take a shot at him. Joe Bob's body fell and Sam was left holding the shotgun by the barrel in one hand and the Model 27 in the other.

Morengeone was gone. He's waiting outside, Sam thought. He'll be at the corner, waiting for me to show my face. Sam stepped toward the door, but he was so concentrated on where Morengeone might be waiting that he tripped on Joe Bob's body and fell, still gripping the shotgun in his left hand. As he hit the floor, he heard the sound of the Cadillac's door slamming. Morengeone had abandoned the fight and was getting away. By the time Sam was on his feet, the Cadillac was smoking rubber on the cement driveway and then roaring across the lawn in a zigzag pattern. Sam watched as the car sped off down the street.

CHAPTER THIRTY-EIGHT

"Nick, is everything O.K. there?"

"Yeah? Why? You got Tim?"

"No. Tim's on his way to the airport. The renegade nigger showed up out here with two pals and tried to kill us. Two are dead and the nigger's on the loose. I'm here with a house full of bullet holes and two dead bodies."

"Okay," Nick said. "Tim got the Audi?"

"Yeah. I've got no car."

"You want me to pick you up?"

"No. Get Janice to the airport. Tim will be in short term parking. Did you get the electronic tickets for them?"

"All done. They're set to get on the plane."

"How much time is there?" Sam said.

"About two hours."

"Can you take Janice to the airport now?" Sam said.

"Yeah. I'll make sure they're O.K., get them in the terminal, and then head over to pick you up," Nick said.

"Good. I'll hide out in the woods near here after I close this place up. I don't want to be here when the cops show up. Call me when you're nearby."

"Good luck," Nick said.

Sam pulled the garage door down and spent the next twenty minutes wiping down surfaces where he or Tim might have touched something. After satisfying himself that he had been reasonably thorough, Sam walked into the field behind Janice's house and deeper into the woods next to the field. Within minutes, he had disappeared into the brush. The house was quiet. There were no sounds or signs of life in any of the other distant houses either.

* * *

An hour later, Nick pulled into the short term parking lot at Pittsburgh International Airport. Within five minutes, he spotted the Audi and pulled into a spot nearby. Tim was in the Audi and appeared to be alone. Nick forced

Janice to hide in the back seat until he confirmed things were as they appeared to be. Ten minutes later he came back with Tim.

"Thank God you're safe," she said, grabbing Tim around the neck.

They embraced for a time, and then Tim said, "You made a mistake. You only gave these guys one million dollars. It should have been two. I should be dead right now."

Nick smiled and said, "You're a hard man to kill."

Janice kissed him again, pulling him into her arms. The three gathered up their bags and walked to the airport. They went to the American Airlines desk and got their tickets for New York, where they would get an international flight to South Africa. Sam had arranged with his South African contacts to take Tim and Janice in, protect them and arrange for safe transport to Europe.

When their bags were checked, Nick walked them to the metal detectors and said goodbye. Janice hugged him and kissed him on the lips, murmuring, "Thank you for giving me back my life. I can never thank you and Sam enough. Please come to visit us in Europe."

"Sounds like a good idea," Nick said.

Nick shook hands with Tim and the two went through the metal detectors and into the secure area of the airport. Nick waved again as they walked to the train that would take them to the boarding area.

On the train, Janice and Tim held hands. They had rediscovered each other. They were in love again.

"I'll be glad when this is over," Janice said.

"Me too. I've got a lot of making up to do. I was so stupid to get involved with that woman. I'm sorry. I can never tell you how much."

"But Tim, you killed her. Did you have to do that? I mean, couldn't we just go away? Why did you have to kill her?"

"Maybe I didn't. I don't know. I was scared. I was afraid she would tell the police I was alive and they would come and arrest us. I don't know."

"I'm so sorry you did that," she said.

"I did it for us," he said.

The train doors opened and the crowds began to funnel out. Tim and Janice walked to their boarding area. Boarding would not begin for fifteen minutes, so Tim got two styrofoam cups of coffee, and they sat in chairs near the boarding gate, occasionally holding hands, smiling and generally feeling glad for a new chance at life.

"Does it seem to you that our lives were so empty before?" Tim said.

"Yes," she answered. "Something was missing. You were always working and I was always pretending to be involved in something that invariably turned out to be not very important."

"Is it different now?" He said.

"Oh Tim, we have a new beginning. New people. New places. New us."

"It's too bad you have to nearly die before you can figure out that there's something wrong with your life. But when you look back at it, it's all so predictable. High pressure job, fancy house, stale relationship with the one person who cares about you, looking for happiness where you can't find it, lying to you and to myself... really, when you think about it, committing suicide," he said.

"We have a new chance now, Tim. Don't dwell on what is past. I'm not. That's all over and we have a new life to begin. Let's just concentrate on that."

Boarding for their plane was called and they got up, allowing the other passengers to go in first, preferring the less congested place at the end of the line. As they stood, watching the others pass through the boarding gate, Tim got a glimpse of a figure in the main thoroughfare, a large black man in a baggage handler's uniform, but with a massive build and a shiny face.

Tim grabbed Janice's arm so firmly that she turned to him in surprise. "Listen to me," he whispered. "He's here. The guy who tried to kill me. He knows we're here. He sees us. I don't know how he got here, but he's here. You get on that plane and don't look back. I'll join you later, but you've got to go. Will you do it?"

"Oh, Tim," she sobbed.

"Will you do it?" He insisted.

"Yes. You'll come after me?"

"I'll come after you, but right now, you've got to get away. No matter what, you get away. If it looks to you like I'm hurt, you get away and get safe. You can help me from South Africa. If you stay, there's no help for either of us. Promise me."

"I promise."

Tim was so intent on his conversation with Janice that he didn't see Morengeone coming up from behind. A large black hand rested on his shoulder.

"Well I be a motherfucker," Morengeone grinned, the yellow fangs showing, "If it ain't the happy couple. I see she done brought you back from the grave."

Morengeone's ordinarily striking visage was even more striking now because of a large white bandage on his left cheek bone, where Sam's .40 caliber slug had stuck in his face.

Tim pushed Janice with a violent shove and instantly turned on Morengeone with his styrofoam cup of coffee and jammed it in his face. Temporarily blinded, scalded, and taken off guard, Morengeone stepped back. Tim's knees were weak, and he didn't know what to do, so he just ran at the large man and hit him headlong with his body and at the same time, grabbed him around the neck. Morengeone was off balance, and when Tim hit him, he fell with Tim's weight on his chest.

People scattered and ran to get out of the way. Others gathered at a safe distance to watch the amazing contest. Airline employees frantically called on cell phones and internal landlines for help. No one wanted to get too close. No one knew what was happening.

On his back, Morengeone instantly rolled to get the dominant position, but Tim held on to Bartholomew's neck, pulling Bartholomew's head with all his might into his own chest and wrapping his legs around Bartholomew's midsection. Once he got on top, Morengeone tried to pry Tim's arms from around his neck by sheer force, but Tim grasped one arm with the hand of the opposite arm, and even Morengeone couldn't break the grip. The first punch to the kidneys did it though. Tim's grip broke and his legs came loose from Morengeone 's midsection. He rolled to the side, curled up in a ball.

Morengeone bent over the fallen man and lifted him up by main force. Holding him at arm's length, Morengeone cocked his right arm to deliver a killing blow to the head when someone behind him yelled, "Hey you." It was an airline employee.

Morengeone stopped, stunned by the shout, and turned to see who it was. Seizing the only opportunity he'd ever have, Tim delivered a straight kick to Morengeone 's groin. Instantly, Morengeone dropped to one knee and released his grip on Tim's shoulder.

Tim's impulse was to run. To run faster than he had ever in his life imagined a person could run. He wanted out of there and he was so scared that he didn't even know where he was or who he was or why this was happening. But he was frozen in space and time. He couldn't move. Then the huge man with the gleaming sweaty black face leered at him and the yellow canine teeth came out. Reflexively, Tim threw another kick as hard as he could, this time at his head. It worked before, maybe it would work again.

It didn't. Morengeone caught the kick with his left, encircled the leg, trapping it, and then delivered a blow to the leg with his right. A collective gasp went up from the crowd when blood shot out of Tim's leg in a stream. The blow had been delivered with a push dagger and it had slashed through the femoral artery. Morengeone threw the leg away from him to avoid the spurting of blood and got painfully to his feet, the bloody dagger still gripped in his right hand.

Tim was on his back, grasping his spurting leg with both hands and moaning. The push dagger still in his hand, Morengeone walked over to the fallen man and delivered a kick to the side of his head rendering him semi-conscious on the floor. Morengeone then knelt down beside him and thrust the dagger into Tim's solar plexus. Instantly, blood stained the middle of Tim's shirt and his eyes rolled back in his head. He was dead. The push dagger stuck upwards in Tim's chest. "This be for Joe Bob and Whipdick, motherfucker," Morengeone hissed.

Still hurting from the kick to the groin, Morengeone looked around, saw Janice was gone, and ran into the crowd of people who were now gathered around the waiting area where he had fought with Tim. No one stood in his way. He began to run toward the side door leading to the runway, where he had come in. Coming towards him, however, were two county policemen, on the run, their hands pressing their dangling service revolvers close to their legs. In a quick decision, Morengeone began waving his hands at them, and when they got in earshot, yelled, "I goin for medical help. The man back there, he hurt bad. Some white dude did it. Got a beard. Bout thirty years old wearing jeans."

One of the cops kept running, the other stayed with Morengeone long enough to radio in the description of the assailant. Then, noticing the blood on Morengeone 's uniform coat, he said, "What's that?"

"Oh," Morengeone said, "I tried to help him. I give him artificial restoration."

"Oh," the cop said, knowing something wasn't right, but not knowing what it was. His instinct told him to cuff this guy and take him on to the scene."

"I get the doctor now," Morengeone said.

The cop hesitated. Get the doctor? Why couldn't he just call it in? He didn't like it. But he had to do something. He needed to catch up to his partner. This guy was suspicious, but he couldn't cuff him without a reason. Besides, he was black. He could hear it now, "You wouldn't have stopped a white guy. But that blood. . . ."

"Okay," the cop said, turning in the direction his companion had gone.

By the time the correct description of the assailant had been broadcast, Morengeone was in his Cadillac cruising down the parkway.

"Nuther day, nuther five grand," he mused.

CHAPTER THIRTY-NINE

Janice called Sam from New York. "We don't know anything yet," Sam said. "Call me again when you get to Johannesburg. I'll know then. Whatever you do, don't miss that plane."

Tim was dead and Sam knew it — all of Pittsburgh knew it — but he wasn't going to tell Janice until she got to South Africa. There he could arrange for someone to be with her. In New York, nothing was set up. If he told her in New York, she might not get on the plane, and by the time they found out who the dead man was and that Janice's house was full of dead bodies and bullet holes, they would be watching for her at any international airport. She had to leave and she had to leave now.

Eighteen hours later she called and Sam told her Tim was dead. Sam had already alerted the South Africans and they had medical help available to counsel her. Grief in a strange land.

A week later, Janice called again.

"Sam, I have transferred another million dollars into your account."

"Why? You've paid what you owe."

"No. Tim wanted you to have it."

"Tim?"

"Yes. It's the first thing he said to me when I saw him at the airport. He said you saved his life and he wanted you to have two million dollars."

"It doesn't work that way, Janice. You paid us and we did the work. That's all. You don't owe us any more money."

"Well, then, that's only part of the reason I've given you this money. I want you to kill the man who had Tim killed."

"Janice, this is something you'll want to think about. It will take you several months before you can sort all of this out."

"You're wrong, Sam. It's sorted out. Do it." She hung up.

CHAPTER FORTY

Nick returned to the Landcruiser, which was parked deep in bushes across the road from the Badersault estate. It was also covered with branches and it was invisible in the early evening light. Sam and Ronin sat near the Landcruiser in deeper bush, waiting. Ronin sensed Nick's approach before Sam knew Nick had returned. He looked at Sam and his tail wagged slightly.

"Okay, big dog," Sam whispered.

Nick appeared in the clearing forty yards distant and Sam clicked his mini light to give him their location. Nick skirted the clearing, staying in the edge of the bush and finally came up on Sam and Ronin. The big dog licked his face. Nick petted him and turned to Sam.

"No electronics. Two men outside. One, maybe two inside. Old beater Cadillac parked outside."

"Bartholomew Morengeone?" Sam said.

"Looks like it."

"Let's go."

The two men and the dog disappeared into the bush. Both wore black clothing, boonie hats, and both had black and green paint on their faces. Sam carried an FN P90 flattop with an ACOG red dot sight. Nick carried an AK 47. Both men had two .45 pistols each. Sam had an LT Wright unmarked black fighting knife taped upside down to a shoulder harness; Nick carried a Becker Extreme with a seven inch blade in S30V. Ronin carried two inch fangs.

Nick led the way once they got across the county road which ran alongside the Badersault estate. The house was back from the road almost half a mile. The first part of the trek was though an open woods, but the tree line stopped a hundred yards from the house and there was only grass between the woods and the shrubbery around the house.

The outside guards were problematic. One of the guards stood near the front door; the other stood fifty yards distant from the house in the middle of the yard with nothing around him.

"We'll have to use Ronin," Nick said. "I'll hit transmit once when I am in position."

"O.K. I'll hit transmit twice when Ronin is going."

"Got it," Nick said.

The two men split up. Nick circled the house toward the rear so that he could approach from the back where there were no guards and then slip alongside the house until he got within striking distance of the guard by the front door. He would use the shrubbery as cover.

Sam and Ronin went along the tree line until they got directly behind the man standing in the middle of the clearing. Ronin had a high frequency transmitter affixed to his collar that would allow him to hear Sam's signal to attack. Sam knelt and watched; Ronin sat and watched. Nick hit the transmit button, signaling that he was in position. Sam watched for a few minutes, and then whispered, "Stalk."

Ronin went into a crouch and crept onto the grass. He moved slowly, like a sniper, a few inches at a time, sometimes more, belly on the ground, toward the man in the yard. The distance was fifty yards. His dark brown and black coloring made him appear to be a mound of grass. Ten minutes later, Ronin was in position. He was flat to the ground, ten yards from his target, frozen in position.

Sam monitored Ronin's progress and Nick waited for Sam's signal. When Ronin came within ten yards of the sentry, Sam pressed the transmit button on their communicators. Nick and Ronin simultaneously heard and both attacked. Nick was crouched behind a shrub, against the house, close to his target, near the front door.

At Sam's signal, Ronin rose to his feet and took off at a silent gallop toward the man, who was facing away from him. The sentry was just beginning to turn when Ronin hit him hard in the middle of the back. On impact, the man's head snapped to the rear and his body fell forward. He dropped his weapon, an AR 15, and tumbled forward with Ronin's teeth locked on his shoulder. Now Ronin was growling, shaking his head, and actually dragging the struggling man partially this way and that, across the lawn. That was the first sound the other sentry heard. The man on the ground was too stunned and confused at first to even make a sound, but within seconds he was shouting and bellowing with terror. He had no idea what had a hold on his shoulder, but it was big and it felt like he would be eaten alive by whatever it was. It flashed through his mind that he was being eaten by a lion.

When Ronin moved, Nick moved too. He knew that the door sentry would see or hear the Ronin attack and would look toward the yard and away from the house. As soon as Ronin hit, the growling started and the door sentry instantly looked and stepped in that direction. Nick was moving at the same time and was on him in four steps, plunging the Becker Extreme into the side of the neck just as the man was raising his weapon and was about to take another step toward the noise.

Sam was moving too. As soon as Ronin struck, Sam ran toward the man and dog locked in combat. Ronin had the man down on his stomach and had plunged his teeth into the man's shoulder. The big dog was growling, shaking his head and tearing the wounds deeper, and actually dragging the man across the lawn. The man was screaming for help. When Sam got to the fallen man, he plunged both knees into the middle of his back, knocking the air out of his lungs, and drove the Wright fighter into the back of the man's neck, pulling downward and back, severing the spinal cord. The sentry instantly went slack.

"Leave it," Sam ordered Ronin.

The big dog reluctantly released the dead man's shoulder. Sam turned the man over and went through his pockets. Car keys, cell phone, wallet. Sam took the cell phone and signaled for Ronin to follow, then moved toward Nick's position.

Sam said, "Any communications gear?"

Nick answered, "No. Cell phone. That's all."

"Same with my guy," Sam said.

"Front door?" Nick said.

"Lets do it." Sam said.

The two moved to the front door and Nick took out his tools. Within a minute and a half, the dead bolt snicked open. Moving cautiously, Nick opened the door and crept inside to a covering position. Sam ordered Ronin to stay in the shrubbery. There was no sign of wiring on the door. Presumably, their presence was still unknown.

They were in a large foyer. A medieval chandelier five feet across hung from a two story vaulted ceiling. The floor was flagstone. Beyond the foyer, there was a large stairway, wide enough for five men to stand on each step. It went up to a landing punctuated by massive stained glass windows, and then wound its way further up.

The stairway itself seemed to be placed in a kind of second foyer, perhaps a place where parties might be held. It was large, extending fifty feet across the front of the house and maybe forty feet deep. Furniture seemed to be lining the walls, tables, chairs, lamps, and clusters of chairs where people might sit and talk, leaving the center of the room empty.

Four sets of doors led out of the large foyer, the two sets to the back of the room probably going to a food service area, the ones to the right and left, each double doors fourteen feet high, probably led to living quarters, perhaps a dining room, perhaps a sitting area.

The house was tomb-like, but there was the faint sound of voices from the left. Very faint. Sam and Nick moved silently in that direction. Nick cracked a huge door open. It was dark inside the room. The dining room. Sam followed Nick into the room, past the massive table and twenty chairs, and towards the next door, heading now toward the back of the house. This door too led to a darkened room, which seemed to be a sort of sitting room with huge leather chairs and couches. On the far side of that room they could see a line of light under the door leading to yet another room, and the sound of voices was more distinct, although still quite muffled.

Sam and Nick crossed the sitting room to the door with the shaft of light under it, and Sam stuck a fiber optic device under the door and held up two fingers, meaning two men were present in the other room, the tops of their heads barely visible above the wingback leather chairs they were seated in next to the fireplace. Nick and Sam waited silently another ten minutes to see whether any other men would appear. None did. There were no other sounds, no other apparent activity in the house, no sign that an alarm had been raised. The two men in the next room continued talking in subdued tones.

Nick led the way into the room, opening the door ever so slowly, an inch at a time until there was enough room for a man to sneak through the opening. It was the library. The two men were in chairs with their backs to Sam and Nick. The fireplace burned warmly against the cool night. Nick moved silently along the outside wall, the one with tall paned windows reaching almost floor to ceiling, as Sam stayed near the door they had come in. When Nick got to the far end of the room, the men in the chairs were between the two intruders, who approached them from different directions and from behind. The two men were facing the fireplace. Sam and Nick began to move toward the fireplace and the men sitting in front of it. They moved silently, in careful, shuffle steps, until they were directly behind the high backed chairs. They could just see the top of Morengeone 's head in the chair ahead of Nick. They could hear Badersault but not see him.

There must have been a slight noise, because Morengeone suddenly vaulted around in his chair, looking backwards with his knee on the cushion. He looked into the barrel of Nick's AK 47.

"Whut the fuck," he exclaimed.

Badersault stood up and looked too. He looked into the barrel of Sam's P90 submachine gun.

"Turn around, both of you, hands behind your head, kneel down," Nick ordered.

"Do it," Sam said, "Or we shoot you where you stand."

Badersault and Morengeone knelt. Nick searched Morengeone, finding a neck knife, a .38 caliber revolver in a pocket, another knife inside a belt sheath, a derringer in a back pocket, and a small automatic in an ankle holster. Sam's search of Badersault turned up a .32 caliber Walther in the pocket of his robe.

As Sam finished the search, a small red glow caught his eye. There was a button on the arm of Badersault's chair which was only visible from the floor, where Sam knelt next to Badersault, and it was glowing red.

"Alarm," Sam said. "He tripped an alarm."

Instantly, one of the far doors burst open and two men came into the room, handguns held at low ready. Nick wheeled and fired a burst from his AK47. Sam rose and shot a fifteen round burst from his P90. Both men slumped to the floor. They had not fired a shot. The smell of cordite was thick in the room and Morengeone and Badersault were nearly deaf with the roaring of the submachine guns. Sam and Nick were protected with electronic noise suppressors in their ears, part of their Active Ear-Defender communication system.

"Cover," Sam said. He moved along the wall toward the downed men, kicked their guns away, and closed the doors they had come through, locking them on the inside with a bolt. Nick stayed with Morengeone and Badersault, who were both prone in front of the fire. Sam then checked the fallen men for a pulse. There was none. Nick covered him as he made the check.

"Any more of them?" Nick hissed to Badersault.

"There are two outside," Badersault said, clearly frightened, his ears ringing from the firing.

"That's it?"

"Yes."

"Where does this alarm go?"

"The kitchen."

"Anywhere else?"

"No."

"Move over to the table and sit," Sam said. "One on each side. Insect, you sit over by the windows."

"Insect?" Morengeone said, "Who you callin insect, Honkey?"

"Do what he says," Nick barked.

"I'll pay you a million dollars not to do this," Badersault said.

"We can only work for one person at a time," Nick answered.

"You might want to reconsider," Badersault smirked.

"Why?" Sam said.

"Can I reach in the drawer at the end of the table?" Badersault said.

"What's in there?" Sam said.

"A contract on your lives," Badersault said. "If you kill me, a million goes to the person who kills you both."

"I'd say you have a problem," Sam said.

"What?"

"It's hard for a dead man to administer a contract," Sam said.

"Not really. My lawyer has it. He gives it to an escrow agent. They pay when the killer proves to them he killed you."

"What's to prevent your lawyer from just walking away with the million?" Nick said.

"Another lawyer monitors him," Badersault said.

"Not bad," Sam said, "But if the second lawyer is smart, he will just call the first lawyer and offer to split the million."

"There are other contracts on the lawyers," Badersault said.

"Byzantine," Nick murmured.

Morengeone fidgeted in his chair, his eyes darting back and forth between the speakers.

"You a tweaker, Morengeone?" Nick said, swinging the barrel of the AK to point at Morengeone .

"Ain't no tweaker," Morengeone said.

"Then stop acting like one," Nick said.

"Here's the bottom line for you, Fritz," Sam said, "You made all these arrangements but you can't rely on any of them because they're all illegal, so no reliable institution will act as escrow agent, and that leaves you relying on low lifes, like Bartholmew over there and your scummy lawyer, and that is a losing proposition."

"You're right," Badersault said, "But it's what I've got."

"How much are you worth?" Sam said.

"I don't know. Hundreds of millions," Badersault said.

"Isn't this a poor way to end up for zillionaire?" Sam mused.

"It isn't what I'd like," Badersault said.

"But you're back on television the other day, ripping off the public again, you and that shit-faced governor," Sam said.

"Yeah, well, Percy, him and me go back a ways," Badersault said. "He hands me the money and I take it."

"Why?" Sam asked. "You don't need it."

"I don't know what else to do," Badersault said. "It's what I do."

"You said you wanted to change," Sam said. "Do something else with your life."

"I can't," Badersault said.

"I know," Sam said.

"Can I show you the contract?" Badersault said.

"Move very slowly," Sam said.

Badersault moved to the end of the table and slowly opened the drawer, extracting a folded document. He placed it on the table and opened it up, revealing a small automatic pistol. With surprising speed, he picked up the pistol and swung it toward Nick, who was standing between him and Morengeone near the windows, when Nick and Sam fired at the same time, ripping Badersault's center of mass to shreds. The pistol fell on the table, free of Badersault's dead hand, and his body danced to the rear and then fell, hit with twenty or more rounds.

When the shooting started, Morengeone catapulted backwards in the chair, landing on his back. He flipped his legs over his head, regained his feet facing the interior of the room, and dove through the window backwards. Landing on some shrubs, again on his back, he zig-zagged his way to his car, which was twenty-five yards from the window. He was in the seat with the door open and the key in the ignition when Ronin caught up to him and sank his fangs into Morengeone's thigh.

"Jesus Christ," he yelled. "Get off. Get the fuck off. I'll kill your furry ass."

But Ronin growled and maintained his grip. The pain in Morengeone's leg was terrific and he was pounding on the dog's head and fumbling to get the car started at the same time. Ronin held on. Blood was beginning to stain Morengeone's pants and the seat. He desperately needed to get away. Finally, he got the car started and began to drive on the lawn, dragging Ronin, who was growling and twisting and digging deeper into his thigh. As soon as the car started moving, Sam blew his silent whistle and Ronin released his grip and scampered free of the car.

Sam and Nick had their sights on the car in case Morengeone decided to try to run over the dog, but he kept going as far away from Ronin as he could get.

Sam picked up the contract Badersault had put on the table and Sam and Nick crawled out the broken window to the yard. Ronin came panting over to them, and the three set off for the woods.

No telling who would be trying to kill them now.